Lessons of Panchatantra
Ratan Lal Basu

Lessons of Panchatantra

Lessons of Panchatantra

Contents

Chapter-1: Vishnu Sharma and His Art of Teaching

Thousands of books and articles have been written on Panchatantra and various aspects of the text, its origin, history etc. have been closely scrutinized by erudite scholars to the best conceivable depths. But here our approach is going to be quite novel. Eschewing all theoretical queries we adopt the story telling mode right from the beginning, as in case of the text of Panchatantra. The story telling mode of presenting any topic has its origin in unknown past and it has been again and again verified that this mode of presenting any topic is the most attractive, effective and the least time consuming mode of instilling any concept into the comprehensive faculty of the target audience or readers. So, let us pass straight on to the introductory story of our presentation of the mysterious text of Panchatantra.

Lord Vishwakarma, the engineer and architect of heaven happened to indulge in the idea of creating intelligent beings, the humans, full of all the virtues and free from the vices – Kama, Krodha, Lobha, Mod, Moha and Matsarya (respectively Desire, Anger Greed, Pride, Obsession and Jealousy). He expected that these pious human beings would worship the deities in heaven and thereby enhance their prowess so as to make them more powerful and efficient against the titans in the eternal war of the gods and the titans. With a view to giving concrete shape to his project, Vishwakarma requested Lord Nandi, the Bull mount of Lord Shiva to supply him the purified souls so that he could endow life to the human bodies created by him. Nandi readily agreed to assist Vishwakarma in this noble project.

The few males and females first created by Vishwakarma and sent to earth started giving birth to children – bodies of the fetuses in the womb being supplied by Vishwakarma and the souls by Nandi. Each human had a life span of 100 years, and as the births were much greater than the deaths, number of humans on earth went on multiplying and they were several hundred in a few years and they spread around to establish new habitations, villages and towns. These human beings from the very birth were devotees of the deities in heaven (actually Nandi instilled this idea in the souls he supplied to Vishwakarma). Lord Vishnu (the one entrusted with the task of preservation of the universe created by Lord Brahma, entrusted with the task of creation, in the Trinity of the Primary Gods) was very much pleased at the worship offerings of the newly created human beings and so he aspired to visit the habitations of these pious beings on earth. With this desire in mind, he, accompanied by his greatest disciple Narada, the sage of the gods, descended on earth in the guise of a Brahmana, Narada being his disciple.

Wherever they went they were treated most courteously as honourable guests and offered sumptuous food and cozy shelter, even the very poor did his best to serve the honoured guests. Vishnu was so pleased that he, after returning to his abode in Baikuntha in the highest level of the heaven, called on Sasthi, the goddess entrusted with births to inspire human beings to give birth to more children. So, the number of humans went on multiplying at accelerating rates and their habitations spread far and wide.

Once again Vishnu undertook to visit human habitations under the guise of a Brahmana and this time too he and Narada were well treated as guests by the humans. So he again instructed goddess Sasthi to take initiative in farther accelerating the growth of human society.

With the utmost efforts of goddess Sasthi, now the rate of birth of human race was so rapid that Vishwakarma had to set up new and larger manufacturing units for human fetus to cope up with the new situation.

But the case was not as simple for Nandi as pure souls could not be produced in assembly line. Each one has to be filtered and purified from vices separately. So Nandi could no longer be scrupulous to his duty and went on supplying unpurified souls to Vishwakarma and thereby the newborn human beings were no longer pure and free from vices. Thus the human society as it spread far and near got corrupted with most of the human beings besmirched with the six basic vices and their complex combinations.

As the puja offerings sent by humans to the gods were now impure and mixed with harmful and dirty elements, Lord Vishnu decided to visit in disguise the human societies once again to find out the reason of this impurity in the puja offerings. As before, he as a Brahmana and Narada as his disciple descended on earth and found that human societies were no longer pure and sacred but corrupted with all the basic vices. As before they approached one household and told that they had been coming from a distant place and therefore tired and hungry. At this the members of the household started to abuse them and chased them away with sticks on the hands of each member of the household. They encountered similar experience everywhere. Examining the human societies, remaining invisible, they found that human society had been divided among rich and poor, a few rich owning all resources and the poor majority serving them as slaves. The society was also dividing into castes, races, religious communities each hating and fighting the others.

Infuriated Vishnu decided to destroy this polluted human race with his wheel weapon (Sudarshana Chakra). But soon his anger calmed down and he thought that it should first be reasonable to consult the gods and the other two members of the Trinity viz., Brahma and Shiva. He first invited the ordinary gods to Vaikuntha and the king of the gods, Indra told him that existence of the human race is essential to keep alive the strength and spirits of the gods along with the trinity. So, it would be better to find some way out to purify the corrupt human societies. As Vishnu could not devise any way out he, along with the gods, went to Kailasha, the abode of Lord Shiva. Shiva also said that he too could not eke out any solution and therefore all of them moved to Brahmaloka and related the matter to Lord Brahma the creator. Brahma said that for persistence of the human race it is necessary that there ought to be basic vices, but it is to be seen that these vices are kept strictly under control and in benign states. At the request of the gods Brahma decided to write a great book containing all teachings to keep the vices under control in human society.

Brahma then with painstaking efforts and deep thinking composed a vast a treatise consisting of a hundred thousand chapters. In it were treated the subject of Virtue, Profit, and Pleasure, which the Self- born designated as the triple aggregate. He treated of a fourth subject called Emancipation with opposite meaning and attributes. The triple aggregate in respect of emancipation, viz., to the attributes of Goodness, Passion, and Darkness, and another, (a fourth, viz., the practice of duty without hope of bliss or reward in this or the other world), were treated in it. Another triple aggregate connected with Chastisement, viz., Conversation, Growth, and Destruction, was treated in it. Another aggregate of six consisting of the hearts of men, place, time, means, overt acts, and alliances, and causes, were treated in it.

From this great book of Lord Brahma, were generated all the following sastras of ancient India written by the Rishis and great scholars.

1. The 4 Vedas: Rigveda, Samveda, Yajurveda and Atharvaveda.

2. 4 Upavedas

i) Ayurveda from Rigveda

ii) Gandharvaveda from Samveda

iii) Dhanurveda from Yajurveda and

iv) Arthasastra from Atharvaveda

3. The Dharmasastras in the form of Sutras (short prose)

4. The Arthasastras

5. The 6 Angas (Sarangas): Yotis, Vyakarana, Chhanda etc.

6. 6 major Philosophies: a) Vedanta of Badarayana, b) Nyaya of Gautama, c) Mimamsa of Jaimini, d) Yoga of Patanjal, e) Samkha of Kapila and f) Vaisesika of Kanada

7. 108 Upanishadas

8. The Epics (Valmiki's Ramayana and Vyasadeva's Mahabharata)

9. Srimad Bhagavad Gita

10. 18 Puranas

11. 36 Up-Puranas

And many other minor sastras and literary texts.

A large number of intelligent persons from the human habitations on earth were trained in all the above subjects by Devi Saraswati, the cohort of Brahmadeva and the goddess of learning. These well trained human teachers, called rishis, were instructed to establish educational institutions in natural surroundings (called Ashramas) to impart knowledge of the sastras on most of the humans since their very youth, and see to it that these knowledge gives them power to have control over the basic vices and instill in them all virtues to live a pious and ethical life with a positive and rational view towards life and society and devotion and respect to gurus (teachers), parents and other elderly persons and above all the celestial deities.

However, the effect of the teachings in this manner on human society as regards purifying it from the vices was only marginal. In fact, teachings of the sastras were time consuming and even if a person starts learning in the Ashramas from his very childhood it takes at least 55 to 60 years for a student to acquire the full wisdom enabling him to live an ethical life with command over the basic vices. So, every person below this age still remained controlled by the vices and human society remained almost at the same level of impurity. So the trinity of the gods conferred and thought of devising some less time consuming method of imparting the knowledge of ideal vice free living by human beings.

To this end, the tri devas summoned all the rishi teachers and arranged for a conference to be attended by these rishis, the tri devas and their cohorts, the king of the gods Indra along with all the gods and goddesses. In the meeting Lord Vishnu requested the rishis to meditate and find out some means to impart the lessons of the sastras in a short and effective span of time.

Returning on earth, the rishis got engrossed in research and meditations so as to devise a method of teaching of the sastras in a short span of time. But none could devise any way out in this regard, that is to impart teaching of the basic lessons of sastras in a very short span of time so that a student is enabled to practise the ethical way of living from his very youth. After ten years of relentless efforts one of the sages hit upon a novel idea. The idea suddenly sprang up in his mind from an incident he happened to encounter in a village. While passing through the village in the evening, the sage came upon a congregation of villagers around an old man under a banyan tree. Getting closer the sage discovered that the old man was telling some story. The story involving animals and elaborated by means of gestures, gesticulations and acting by the speaker was so interesting that the sage could not but listen to the story till the end and he discovered also that through the metaphor of the animals the old man endeavoured to instill in the minds of the audience some moral concepts. The sage leapt up in joy and on his way back he thought that he had ultimately found out the method of disseminating the essential aspects of the sastras in the most effective way and in course of a very short span of time. So he decided to write attractive stories embodying all the essential knowledge pertaining to ethics of the sastras. In fact, this method was a very ancient method, invented by Narada, the sage of the heaven. But application of this method was confined mainly among the gods and that too in a very limited way. Some of these stories however, had dropped down to human society in a scattered way and covering only limited topics and sometimes used to impart morals to villagers by old wise men as was the case of that evening-gathering in the village on his way. Now the sage collected many such stories, folklores, fairy tales, examined them closely and thereafter he started composing his own stories. He followed the styles of the stories he had read and extended the coverage of the stories so as to embrace all the essential lessons of the sastras relevant to decent and ethical living.

The sage teacher was endowed with talent and imagination and artistic attributes so as to organize all the stories he had composed into a coherent and unified structure – a complex and well defined structure to serve his specific purpose. He expected that these stories were likely to delight not only children but also people of all ages, from all walks of life.

The sage teacher wrote down the completed text in five (pancha) parts (tantra) and therefore gave it the name Panchatantra and wrote the entire text on dried and processed palm leafs (the only material to write on in those days), made five copies of the original and submitted them respectively to each of Lord Shiva, Lord Vishnu, Brahmadeva, Indra, the king of the gods, and the other sages. The Trinity and all other gods went through the absorbing stories and were very much impressed by the ingenious creation of the sage. This sage author along with other sage teachers was summoned to a meeting of the gods in Vaikuntha, the abode of Vishnu. While asked how long it would take to impart teaching through these stories, the composer sage replied that it would be six months to one year. But nothing could be definitely said unless it is tested and confirmed by means of application in practice. The meeting unanimously came to the conclusion, even before practical testing, that the work was as powerful and penetrating as the war-wheel (Sudarshana Chakra) of Lord Vishnu. So the author was unanimously given the name Vishnu Sharma.

Vishnu Sharma returned to earth and started travelling far and wide to find out any opportunity to test the efficacy of his method of teaching – to find suitable young students willing to take lessons on the essential aspects of the sastras for decent and pious living and to become good and ideal rulers, i.e. to acquire practical wisdom related to living and ruling in an ethical and virtuous manner. After several years of travel he arrived at a beautiful and prosperous city called Mahilaropya. The splendour of the city made Vishnu Sharma spellbound. The high rise mansions with exquisite architectural designs surrounded by ponds with crystal clear water, gardens embellished with flowers and fruits, the wide and clean highways shadowed by lush green foliage, and above all the royal palace almost outmatching the palace of Indra in heaven mesmerized Vishnu Sharma. He learnt from the local people that it was the royal palace of Amara Shakti, the king of the country. While Vishnu Sharma was examining, the architectural novelty of the royal palace with pillars of exquisite designs and embellished with priceless jewels, from a place close to the entrance of the palace, the guards of the palace took him, from his shabby and tattered garments (a consequence of relentless journey), to be a vile person with some sinister motive and was at the point of arresting him while an angry loud voice "stop" made them puzzled as it was the voice of no less a person than Sumati, one of the most trusted ministers of the king. Sumati promptly came forward and at the utter astonishment of the guards offered pranam to the beggar-like person touching his feet and with smile and in a polite tone he said, "Guruji do you recognize me?" Vishnu Sharma too was astonished to find his erstwhile favourite student at this unexpected place. Before he could ask any question Sumati said that he was now a minister of the king of the country. He then said, "It appears that you are very tired after a long journey. So let us first go to my house and after your bath, meditation, meals and rest, we would relate our stories to each other."

He ordered the guards to look for some official so as to arrange for a palankin for his guru to accompany him to his house.

Sumati, with his wife, son and daughter, performed all the rituals customary for accepting a guru to a disciple's house. After bath, Vishnu Sharma wore the newly purchased garments suitable for him. He then performed the usual worship of Lord Shiva, Vishnu ant other deities.

Thereafter he took only some fruits and milk as lunch (he did not eat anything else). After some rest he told Sumati everything from the very beginning of the meeting of the gods. Confirmed by his guru about his newly invented teaching method Sumati got very much elated as at that very moment he had been looking exactly for this. He then related to his guru how through painstaking efforts, diligence, dedication and honesty and above all, by the blessings of his guru and the gods he could raise himself from the position of a low level royal employee to the position of a very important minister of the king. He then said, "Guruji, I have already heard from some people of the novel method of teaching you have invented at the behest of Lord Vishnu and other gods. In fact, I was just thinking of proceeding to your Ashrama in this regard while by god's grace I found you right at the palace gate being harassed by the keepers." In utter surprise Vishnu Sharma asked, "For which reason it was necessary for you to meet me at my Ashrama."

In his reply, Sumati gave the detail of the circumstances which had compelled him to look for his guru. Amara Shakti was a very able and wise king and prosperity and happiness made his kingdom the best one in human society. Still the king had an anxiety that after his relinquishing the throne there would be none to be a proper ruler as all the three of his sons – Vasu Shakti, Ugra Shakti and Ananta Shakti were ignorant and completely averse to learning. They indulged only in playing, gambling, merry making, hunting and many other deeds which are not befitting the princes, especially the sons of such a wise and ideal king like Amara Shakti. All the teachers appointed to teach the princes for the last few years failed to generate even an iota of interest in them about learning. So, at last the king summoned the ministers and asked for their advice. While the other ministers failed to give the king any meaningful advice, Sumati suddenly remembered his guru who he had heard, had discovered some novel method of teaching and it was so ingenious that he was honoured with the title of Vishnu Sharma after the name of Lord Vishnu. Sumati had immediately related the matter to the king who requested Sumati to somehow convince his guru to come to this city and undertake to teach his refractory sons. So Sumati had decided to meet his guru at his Ashrama, but fortunately the desired person had already come to the palace gate by the grace of the gods.

The next day Sumati took his guru along to the royal court and introduced him to the king and the other ministers. Everybody bowed to him and offered him pranam as they had already heard the name of this great sage blessed by all the gods and bearing the name of Lord Vishnu. The calm and pious demeanor and deep penetrating intelligent looks of the sage alone gave confidence to the king and others in the royal court that he would be the real teacher to bring the wayward princes under control. Then the king bowed and asked politely, "Guruji, how long would it take to give my sons the basic and essential teachings of rational and pious living and of practical but ethical norms of politics, economics and other subjects essential for an ideal ruler?" Vishnu Sharma replied politely, "That I would tell you after I have talked with your sons privately."

An official then ushered the teacher to the room of the three princes. Vishnu Sharma, as he has already expected, found the boys gossiping, laughing loudly, drinking and gambling. As Vishnu Sharma and the official entered the room, they got very much irritated and said loudly, "Who has permitted you to make this old man enter our room and spoil our games?" The official replied politely, "Your father has sent him and he would henceforth be your teacher." The boys started laughing loudly and making humiliating remarks about the new teacher. The official left and ignoring their remarks Vishnu Sharma started to initiate talks with them. After half an hour the king himself came and peeped into the room and was surprised to find the princes turned docile, which they had never done with the earlier teachers, and were listening attentively the sage teacher. After two hours Vishnu Sharma came out to the court keeping the princes spell bound as though mesmerized and declared that he would take only six months to impart on his students all the essential knowledge as embedded in all the sastras of ethics, morality, practical economics and politics, ideas necessary for all conceivable professions including that of the ruler, ministers and high government officials.

The ecstatic king declared openly that if the teacher is successful, he would offer him a vast part of his kingdom and immense wealth. Vishnu Sharma smiled politely and said, "Reverend King, I am now eighty and have already become free from all worldly desires. I need nothing more than some milk and fruit to keep myself alive, a simple bed of mat in a straw cottage and a small noise free place to perform my worship. What can I do with land, wealth or jewel? So, you need not pay me any remuneration for teaching your sons. You rest assured that your sons would become wise having capacity to be ideal rulers in six months. If, however, I fail, I would give up teaching altogether and go into complete seclusion. Moreover, it is you who is to be thanked as you have given me the opportunity to test the efficacy of my novel teaching method."

Vishnu Sharma was successful and the magic stories behind his success are embedded in the great treatise, the story book for all ages, occupations, countries, races, religious communities and so on – the Panchatantra. So, it is time to enter the magic world of Panchatantra.

In this work, the stories are presented in five Tantras (parts). Each Tantra consists of a primary story and a complex structure of inter-woven secondary stories have been formed to bring to the fore the essence of the primary story. In the complex structure of the secondary stories, stories within stories may be of several stages. If a character of a story tells a story to substantiate his view, then we name this as "sub-story". If there are further stories within a sub-story, we would call this "chain-story" and similarly there may be stories within a chain-story, i.e. chain-story-2. For example if A tells a story to B and in this story a character say C tells a story to D, this is a sub-story. Now, if in this sub-story a character, say E tells a story, this is a chain story of stage-I and so on.

Chapter-2: Tantra I-Breaking off of Friendship

Primary Story: The Bull Sanjivaka and the Lion Pingalaka

With a view to trying his luck in foreign trade, a merchant named Vardhamana undertook to travel with merchandise loaded in caravans drawn by two sturdy bulls called Nandana and Sanjivaka. Unfortunately, in the midst of the forest, the bull Sanjivaka was caught in mud and severely injured. Entrusting some servants the responsibility of looking after the injured bull the merchant continued his journey. However, the unscrupulous servants left the injured bull at large and meeting the merchant declared that the bull had died of injury. It was good fortune for the bull that soon he recovered, and being nourished by rich grass of the forest, soon became stout and vigorous and his loud bellowing frightened the lion Pingalaka, the king of the forest. Two jackals, Damanaka and Karataka, sons of two ministers and jobless, had been aspiring to please the king somehow and get the jobs of ministers in the court of the king. The Bull incident gave them an opportunity to come closer to the king. Of the two jackals, Karataka was docile and conscientious and never liked to indulge in unfair and hideous means to get into power. But the other jackal, Damanaka, was mad for power and by nature he was unscrupulous to the hilt and for getting into power he was ready to adopt all conceivable means, fair or foul. Examining the horrifying sound, Damanaka could realise that it was simply the bellowing of a bull and so he convinced Pingalaka that it was but a grass eating benign animal. Through his initiative a deep friendship developed between Pingalaka and Sanjivaka.

But this friendship ultimately turned out to be disastrous for both the jackals and other animals of the forest as the absorbing friendship of the lion with the wise bull made him oblivious of all his royal duties.

So, the jackals decided to break the friendship. Damanaka took the major initiative in this regard and hatched up a heinous conspiracy in order to get his purpose served. He talked separated with the lion and the bull and through insinuation tried to turn friendship into deep-seated mutual distrust and enmity. Unfortunately the lion unlike an ideal and rational king took the jackal (who had been away from royal court for a long time and about whose actual nature and motives the lion had no knowledge) into confidence and started believing as the jackal had said that the bull was conspiring to kill him. For the bull, the allegation against the lion was not difficult to gulp as he knew that a bull is a natural fodder animal for a lion. The mischievous efforts of the cunning jackal came to fruition, resulting ultimately in a fight between Pingalaka and Sanjivaka in which Sanjivaka was killed and Pingalaka was fatally injured.

So the dirty conspiracy of unscrupulous and cunning Damanaka brought about a greater disaster to the forest kingdom and all its citizens.

Lessons: i) An ideal king should never be emotional and do anything in the spur of the moment.

ii) An ideal king ought not to be gullible and should never be moved by the advice of a single person and he should discuss any report by someone with all his ministers and scrutinize the advice himself calmly and applying political prudence. The king should always be cautious about deceitful advice.

iii) An ideal king should never budge from his royal duties and should never indulge in friendship, games, gambling or any such things that makes him negligent about his royal duties.

iv) An ideal king should never behave like a coward and get panicked at anything strange or unusual as did Pingalaka by hearing the loud and strange bellowing of Sanjivaka.

v) Friendship between natural enemies, e.g. between a lion and a bull is not realistic and may not last long.

vi) Unfair and conspiratorial means to achieve power ultimately leads disaster for the conspirator as well as everyone else.

vii) Seven evils that a monarch may be afflicted with: women, dice, hunting, drinking, abusive speech, rapine and imparting unreasonable severe punishment on any subject. These seven evils together are called addiction. The other fundamental evils that a king may be subjected to are: absence or lack of six requisites (ministers, land and subjects, fortresses, treasury, allies and punitive power).

Secondary Stories

1. The Wedge and Disaster of the Over-curious Monkey

Karataka to Damanaka

In a temple under construction at the border of a forest, the artisans used to take their lunch break at midday for a few hours while a troop of monkeys used to play at the construction site. One noon while leaving for lunch a carpenter left a haft split vast log and supported the cleft at the open end of the log by inserting a wooden wedge inside the cleft. That day too, after the workers had left for lunch, the monkeys came and started playing around the site as usual. A silly monkey got much curious by observing the peg inside the cleft of the log and started examining and finally pulling hard at the wedge. After some frantic efforts he could manage to displace the wedge and unfortunately, as the wedge had been dislodged, the open end of the log snapped shut crashing the lower part of the body of the silly monkey resulting in his instant death.

Lessons: i) One ought not to poke his nose into a matter which is none of his business.

2. The Cautious Jackal and the Battle Drum

Damanaka to Pingalaka

A hungry jackal, frantically looking for food, entered a forest and god terrified by a strange and earsplitting sound coming from some place not far from him. He thought it to be the war cry of some deadly demon and decided to flee away in no time. But soon his courage revived and he decided to examine the source of the horrible sound keeping hidden under bushes. So he started moving towards the source of the sound always remaining under the cover of the bushes. While he had reached the end of the forest he was amazed to find in the open field by the forest a vast war drum which could have been left by some warring parties at the end of some battle and the horrible sound was generated while the leaning long grasses being struck by air brushed against the drum. Knowing the secret of the fearful sound the jackal approached the drum, tore the skin cover at one side of the drum with his teeth and entered the drum expecting some food inside. However, he had to be disappointed.

Lessons: i) One should not get terrified by sound alone, before inspecting the exact cause and nature of the source of the sound, however strange and horrific it seems to be.

3. The Merchant Dantil and Gorambha, the Sweeper of the King's Palace

Damanaka to Sanjivaka

Dantil, the governor of the city named Vardhamana, was much in favour of the king. However, an inadvertent act on his part, being unaware of the real power of the apparently insignificant sweeper of the king's palace put him to intricate jeopardy. At the conclusion of the marriage ceremony of his daughter, when all the guests including the king had left, Gorambha, the sweeper of the king's palace took his seat on an empty chair which was not meant for a person of his status. At this Dantil got furious and forced the sweeper out of his house after humiliating him with harsh words. This severely injured the sentiment of the poor sweeper who resolved to take revenge against Dantil for this utter humiliation. He had been entrusted with the responsibility of sweeping the king's bed room at dawn while the king used to be half awake. He took this opportunity as a means to hatch conspiracy against Dantil. One day while he was sweeping and the king was half awake, the sweeper muttered in low sleepy tone, "what a matter of shame, I found Dantil in deep embrace with the queen". Hearing this the king jumped up and while enquired the sweeper said that he had been sleepy because of gambling last night and so he could not remember what he had uttered in a dozing condition. The king thought that people are likely to speak the truth while drunk or in half-sleep. Therefore, he first debarred the entry of Dantil into the royal palace and gradually deprived him of all high positions he used to enjoy through royal favour.

At first, the merchant was at a loss as to the real cause of the king's disfavour to him, but after thorough enquiry he could ultimately discover that it was due to the revenge of the sweeper for his humiliation in his house during the marriage ceremony of his daughter. So Dantil immediately met the sweeper, apologized to him and pleased him with valuable gifts. Thereafter the sweeper consented to do his best so that the king's favour on the merchant is restored. The next day, while sweeping the king's bed room, the sweeper uttered in sleepy voice, "How funny! I have seen the king eating cucumber while sitting in the toilet." This made the king realize that the sweeper, in half sleep, always mutters nonsense. Thus his earlier statement about the queen and the merchant must be sheer nonsense. So he corrected his mistake by restoring Dantil to all positions he had been deprived of.

Lessons: i) Nobody should ignore the power of a person of lowly status if he has close access to a powerful person. Ignoring and humiliating such persons may bring about disaster.

4. The Ascetic and the Rogue Disciple
Damanaka to Karataka

An ascetic named Devasharma lived alone in a sanctuary and occasionally attended religious rites of the clients as the officiating priest. He soon amassed lucrative wealth in the form of jewels bought by the money obtained by selling the priestly-fees and gifts from the clients. He kept these jewels in a satchel tucked for safely in his waist by covering the satchel by a piece of cloth with binding threads. He was very cautious of his wealth and never parted with it. However, a rogue somehow learnt about the jewels and was determined to steal them by some foul means but refraining from serious crimes like murder. He met the ascetic and by deceitful talks could convince the latter that he had become, even at that young age, disinterested in mundane affairs and got interested in having knowledge of spiritualism by becoming a disciple of the ascetic. The ascetic accepted him as a disciple but he had to sleep outside the sanctuary as religious protocol but did not permit a disciple to sleep inside the sanctuary as that was against religious custom. So the rogue had to sleep outside the sanctuary. By serving the ascetic in various ways the rogue could gain the full confidence of the ascetic, but still he failed to device any safe means of robbing the jewels. However, soon the opportunity came as though by windfall. Being invited by a client to be the officiating priest of a religious ritual in his house, the ascetic decided to take the rogue along while undertaking the long journey to the house of the client. In course of the journey, while they were close to a river, the ascetic felt deep urge for clearing his bowels. He opened his robe, hid the jewel-satchel inside it and entrusting the robe to his trusted disciple looked for some suitable nook for answering the call of nature. Thereafter the ascetic could find a grove suitable for answering the biological urge.at some distance.

After completion of his answer to nature's call, he washed his hands and feet in the river and returning to the earlier spot discovered with utter dismay that his disciple had fled with the robe along with the satchel containing the jewels He could now realize his great folly of attaching so much trust to someone who had been a stranger to him only a few months ago.

Lesson: i) One should never trust anyone, especially a newly acquainted person, while it involves matters related to treasures, property or wealth.

Inside story-1: The Fighting Rams and the Greedy Jackal
(Devasharma, the ascetic, observed while defecating)

Two rams were found to be fighting vehemently and blood dripped around the place where the two struck at each other. After each encounter they drew back to some distance and once again ran fast to crash headlong. Being enticed by the stream of blood a greedy jackal entered the spot and began to savor the blood while the rams moved backwards and withdrew as soon as the rams moved forward. Unfortunately, after some such encounters, the rams moved towards each other so fast that before the jackal could get out safely he was caught between the clashing foreheads and horns of the rams and was crushed to death.

Inside story-2: The Unfaithful Wife of the Weaver and the Silly Go-between

The ascetic Devasharma, bereft of his treasure, felt miserable and as night fell he could fortunately get shelter for the night in the house of a kind weaver. The weaver let her wife take the Ascetic to his house and arrange for his night stay informing her that it would be late for him to return home. The wife took home the ascetic, arranged for his sleep in a cot and decided to meet her lover taking advantage of the long absence of her husband as the latter had already declared. Unfortunately, being dead drunk, the weaver returned home earlier and caught the unfaithful wife red handed while she had dressed up for going out to meet her lover. The angry weaver tied his wife with a rope and fell fast asleep as a result of drinking. Meanwhile the wife of a barber and a close friend of the weaver's wife entered their house, and after learning everything from her tied friend she untied the rope. Then she took the place of the weaver's wife and created opportunity for the latter to enjoy love with her lover expecting that the drunken weaver would not wake from sleep before morning. Unfortunately, while his wife was away enjoying with her lover, the sleep of the weaver broke all of a sudden and in half sleep he called his wife by name in order to apologize for his harsh behaviour to her. Apprehending that her voice could be recognized by the weaver, the barber's wife did not reply.

This made the weaver angry again. In drunken condition he could not recognise the barber's wife and considering her to be his own obstinate wife, cut off her nose severely making her unconscious. Then again he fell asleep. After full enjoyment of love game the weaver's wife returned home and send her injured friend to the latter's home. In the morning, while the weaver was full awake, he was surprised to find his wife free and her nose intact. She convinced her husband that this was done by god because of her chastity and faithfulness to her husband. Thus she could easily fool her husband.

On the other hand, the barber's wife too could fool her husband and make everyone believe that it was her husband who, out of anger, had cut off her nose. The barber was arrested and taken to the judges for his mischief. The ascetic had been sleepless all the night and observed everything. So, while the judges were at the point of sentencing the innocent barber, the ascetic entered the court and gave detail of what had actually happened. Then the judges promulgated that the ears too of the mischievous wife of the barber be cut off.

Lesson of the two Inside Stories: i) A go-between whether to take advantage of fight between two warring parties, or to assist any mischievous activity, or in other matter not related to his own business is likely to encounter doom.

5. The Crow and the Vicious Snake

Damanaka to Karataka

In a vast banyan tree a crow and his wife made their nest and started living happily. Soon the hen crow laid eggs. When the offsprings came out of the eggs the couple were very happy. But their happiness did not last long as a vicious snake, residing in a crevice in the tree, devoured all the offsprings. Being helpless against the powerful enemy the hen crow advised her husband that they should leave the tree and get settled at some safe place. But the husband thought of consulting his jackal friend as regards some alternative. Hearing everything the jackal said that although physically less powerful, the crow could bring about destruction of the serpent by applying intelligence. According to his advice the crow snatched a costly necklace from the house of the king and started flying slowly towards the banyan tree with the king's men chasing the crow with the necklace in his beak. Entering into the tree the crow dropped the necklace into the hole where the serpent resided. The king's men climbed up the tree and rescued the necklace from the hole of the snake after killing it. Thus the crow could revenge the mischief of the serpent and also made their nest safe by applying intelligence.

Lessons: i) A physically weaker person ought to resort to intelligence instead of physical strength to overpower a physically stronger enemy. Where physical vigor fails intelligence may provide a viable way out.

ii) It is always helpful to seek advice from an intelligent friend.

5a. The Crab and the Greedy Crane

Sub Story: Told by the jackal in the main story to the crow seeking his advice

An old crane being incapable of catching fish from a lake thought of a cunning device to devour the fishes without much effort. He feigned to be miserable and by shrewd maneuvering could convince the fishes of the lake that he had learnt from a reliable source that a group of fishermen would soon use vast nets to catch all the fishes of the lake. Thus as he would not be able to catch any fish from the fishless lake, he would have to die of hunger and this thought had made him morose. He assured the panicked fishes that he could save their lives by carrying them in his beak to a distant safe lake. He then started carrying the gullible fishes one by one and eating them after carrying them to a flat plateau. At last he decided to eat the flesh of the crab of that lake and get out of the boredom of eating fish-flesh day in and day out. The crab too was waiting for his turn to be carried to a safe place. As before, the greedy crane carried the crab to his eating place. Seeing the thorns and skeletons of the dead fishes the crab could realize the real intention of the crane and before the crane could kill him, he firmly grabbed the neck of the crane with his sharp claws and beheaded the mischievous crane. He returned after a long journey to the original lake and informed about the vicious designs of the crane. Thereafter, the crab and the remaining fishes went on living safely in the lake.

Lessons: i). Excessive Greed leads to doom.

ii). Nobody should trust his natural enemy.

6. The Lion Mandamati and the Cunning Hare

Damanaka to Karataka

In a forest there lived a crazy and powerful lion who, out of pride, had been killing other animals of the forest indiscriminately. To find a way out of this disastrous activity of the crazy lion, the other animals convened a meeting and unanimously took the decision that they would send one animal to the lion for his daily food and convince him of not killing animals indiscriminately. Thereafter they met the lion and could convince him that indiscriminate killing would soon make the forest animal less leading to starvation of the lion himself. Since then every noon an animal used to sacrifice his life by presenting himself at a specific spot to be the prey of the lion.

When it was the turn of an intelligent hare, he contrived a very cunning device not only to save his own life but also to make all animals free from the menace of the wicked lion. That day, he deliberately went to the appointed place very late. At this the lion got very angry. While asked about the cause of his audacity of coming late, the hare said that it was because of another lion who claims himself as the real king of the forest and had invited Mandamati to fight with him. Furious Mandamati ordered the hare to show the other lion whom he would kill immediately. The cunning hare led Mandamati to a well and told that seeing Mandamati the other lion out of fear had took shelter inside the well. Looking into the well Mandamati mistook his own image to be the audacious other lion and jumped into the well to kill it and in this way he himself got drowned and killed.

Lessons: i) Intelligence is always more powerful than physical prowess and intelligence is likely to help to find a way out of any predicament.

7. The Weaver in Lord Vishnu's Guise and the Charming Princess

Damanaka to Karataka

A weaver along with his chariot maker friend was passing along the street by the royal palace in a city. All of a sudden he caught a glimpse of the princess leaning out from the balcony of the royal palace. The heavenly beauty of the princess made the weaver lose his head and he felt an uncontrollable desire for the princess. His friend, the chariot make, was astonished to learn about the irrational and impossible desire of the weaver and did his best to dissuade the weaver from this unimaginable desire. But the weaver had got so much obsessed with the passion to get the princess at any cost that it seemed impossible to restore his mind to rationality. Returning home when the chariot maker realised that his friend might even commit suicide unless he gets the princess as his soul mate, the chariot maker, being an extraordinary genius in his craftsmanship, designed a mechanical chariot imitating Gadura, the king of the birds and mount of Lord Vishnu. He got his friend dressed up in such a way that the latter resembled Lord Vishnu. He taught his friend how to operate the mechanical bird for flying. Then as instructed by his friend, the weaver on his machine bird flied into the room of the princess at midnight. Before the terrified princess could shriek the weaver declared that he was Lord Vishnu and he had fallen in love with the Princess because of her heavenly beauty and he, therefore, was willing to marry her secretly. The princess, considering this to be a boon, consented to marry the weaver in the guise of Lord Vishnu, through Gandharva marriage ritual. According to this marriage ritual two lovers can get married by means of making love in secret. The weaver left at dawn and used to come every night to enjoy his wife. In the meantime the king and the queen, through spies, learnt about the secret marriage of their daughter with Lord Vishnu and they too considered this to be a heavenly blessing. This king was a vassal king of the Emperor to whom he had to pay annual taxes. This time, however, when the men of the Emperor came to collect the taxes, the king, out of the pride of being the father in law of Lord Vishnu, declined to pay taxes declaring him to be an independent and fully sovereign king. This audacity on the part of a subordinate king infuriated the Emperor who, with a powerful army invaded the kingdom of the delinquent vassal king. The king now requested his son in law, Lord Vishnu, to fight and defeat the invading emperor. With a view to defending his honour and dignity the weaver, who had no power of the Lord Vishnu, intended to fight and sacrifice his life in the battle. The news reached the ears of Lord Vishnu who though that if the fake Vishnu is killed in the battle, people would consider this to be the weakness and death of real Vishnu. This would make people averse to worship of him. So in order to preserve his status, Lord Vishnu instilled divine power in the mechanical bird and the fake fighting wheel (Sudarshana Chakra) of the weaver. So, the weaver could defeat the entire army of the Emperor and took him into captivity.

Lessons: i) Extraordinary strong will and determination may move even the gods of the heaven.

8. The Grateful Animals and the Ungrateful Man
Damanaka to Pingalaka

Yajnadeva, a poor Brahmana, left home in quest of earning. On his way through the forest, he came upon a well and found a tiger, a monkey, a snake and a man captivated at different stages inside the deep well. At the request of them and with the oath from them that they would not do the Brahmana any harm and, on the contrary, pay back his help if he helped them to come out of the well, the Brahmana collected a strong branch of a tree and with the help of it started pulling out the victims one by one from various stages of the well. After the tiger, the monkey and the snake had come out of the well, they requested the Brahmana not to pull out the man, as they knew that he was a wicked person. The tiger and the monkey gave the Brahmana the directions of their houses and requested him to visit their houses so that they could repay their indebtedness. The snake promised if the Brahman remembers the snake while in any trouble, he would appear instantly and rescue the Brahmana.

At first the Brahmana took the advice of the three animals seriously and decided to leave the place without pulling out the man. But continuous request of the man at last raised sympathy in the mind of the good natured Brahmana. So he ignored the warnings of the three benevolent friends, and he collecting a longer branch from a tree and pulled out the man from the lowest level of the well. The man thanked the Brahmana for his help, told that he was a goldsmith and requested the Brahmana to meet him at his residence at Bhrigukaccha if he was in need of any business related to gold ornaments.

The Brahmana, after a few days, could find out the tree where the monkey lived. The monkey was very glad to find his rescuer from the well and presented him with plenty of delicious fruits. Thereafter the Brahmana, on the basis of directions given by the tiger, could find out his cave. The tiger too was glad to find the Brahmana and presented the latter gold ornaments which he had obtained after killing and devouring a prince who had lost his way in the forest. Now the Brahmana met the goldsmith at Bhrigukaccha and requested him to arrange for the sales of the ornaments. The goldsmith could recognise the ornaments which he himself had made for the prince of the kingdom. Knowing fully well that the Brahmana had obtained the ornaments from the tiger, the wicked goldsmith wanted to put him into trouble. He requested the Brahmana to take some rest and, under the pretext of finding some buyer, he went out with the ornaments to the royal palace and reported to the king that the Brahmana had killed the prince and robbed these ornaments. The king's men led by the goldsmith arrested the unlucky Brahmana and threw him into prison in order to execute him the next day. The helpless Brahmana then remembered the snake and as promised the snake immediately appeared into the prison cell. Learning about the cause of imprisonment of the innocent Brahmana, the snake assured him that he would rescue him soon from this grave predicament. He told the Brahmana, "I shall bite the queen to death and because of my divine power nobody could save the queen. Then you would get the opportunity to save her as a simply touch from you would make her free from all venom and revive her to life. And then the king would surely set you free and reward you." Thereafter the snake sneaked into the bedroom of the queen and bit her to death. All classes of snake bite healers failed to restore the queen to life. Then the king announced that anyone who could save the life of the queen would be highly rewarded. Hearing this, the Brahmana told the prison guards that he could heal the queen. He was released and taken to the queen and to utter surprise of everybody, the queen became alive as soon as the Brahmana touched her foot with his finger. Then the king listened attentively to the story of the Brahmana. Thereafter the treacherous goldsmith was put to prison and the Brahmana was rewarded with 100 villages, and a vast amount of wealth. He was also made the prime minister of the king.

Lessons: i) One should not ignore the good advice of benevolent friends.

9. Mandabisarpini, the Bedbug and the Stranger Insect
Damanaka to Pingalaka

A bedbug called Mandabisarpini used to live undetected with her family and relations inside the creaks of folds of the cozy bed of a king. All bugs were very cautious so that none could guess about their existence inside the bed of the king. To this end they used to suck blood from the body of the king very slowly and mildly only when he was in deep slumber and unable to feel the bites of the bugs. One day a strange flying and blood sucking insect happened to be carried by wind through the open window into the room of the king. As the king was not in the room the bugs had come out on the outer layer of the bedstead. The new insect soon made acquaintance with the bugs who, being of simple heart, disclosed the reason of their good health. At this the new insect felt an urge to test the blood of the king. So he sought permission of Mandabisarpini to have shelter inside the folds of the bed so that he too could savor the delicious and nourishing blood of the king. The kind hearted bug permitted inadvertently this insect of unknown character to stay with the bugs. She, however, warned the insect that he should not suck blood unless the king is in deep slumber. But by nature the insect lacked patience and so he bit the king as soon as he got into bed. The king jumped up in pain and loudly called out his men to inspect the bed and see what had bitten him. Under this situation the insect flied out of the window and while the king's men examined the bed thoroughly they could find out the bugs and killed them all.

Lessons: i) One ought not to give shelter to a stranger about whose character one has no knowledge.

10. Predicament of the Indigo Coloured Jackal

Damanaka to Pingalaka

A jackal called Chandarava while chased by dogs in the city happened to fall into the indigo filled drum of a washerman. After the dogs had dispersed, the jackal came out cautiously of the drum and started moving towards his abode inside the forest. On the way he happened to have a glimpse of his image in a pond and was amazed to find himself turned blue and beyond recognition. As soon as he entered the forest every animal who happened to come upon him attempted to flee seeing this strange ferocious looking animal. The cunning jackal could understand the reason of their fear and mildly announced that he would not do them any harm. He further declared that he had been sent by god to rule the animal kingdom as their divine king. Henceforth, the blue jackal on the throne had been living happily, all his food being supplied by other animals. He created various royal positions starting from ministers down to the lower levels of officials.

He put all animals to various royal posts but not any single jackal (his class) got any government post. The aggrieved jackals could soon discover from the attitude and movements of Chandarava that he was but one of their own class, only being painted blue. They knew that a jackal could not resist joining the chorus of howling of jackals. They made a plan to unmask the imposter king, the blue jackal. To this end they, according to plan, gathered close to the throne in the evening and started howling in chorus. Hearing this, the blue jackal forgot everything and joined the chorus in a joyous mood. Discovering that a cunning jackal had fooled them, the enraged animals in the court of the fake king attacked and killed him.

Lessons: i) One if happens to get into high position ought not to neglect ordinary persons who had been close to him before he was raised to power.

11. The Owl and the Wild Goose

Sanjivaka to Damanaka

By a beautiful lake lived a wild goose. One day an owl came to the place and soon made friendship with the goose. The friendless goose was very happy to get a friend although a stranger. After a few days' stay the owl left for his own abode. Before leaving he gave the goose the direction of his abode requesting him to make a visit to his place whenever convenient. A few months after the owl had left, the goose felt lonely and so he decided to make a visit to the residence of the owl. After a long flight as directed by the owl and searching, the goose could ultimately find out the abode of the owl in a large cleft of a vast tree by another lake. It was almost nightfall and the owl could see the goose. He was very happy at the visit of his new friend. The goose too accepted the request of the owl to stay in his residence for a few days. Two days later, a group of merchants laid tents below the tree for night stay. Next dawn they closed the tents and packed up their belongings to start the day's journey again. At that time the owl being a nocturnal bird was still awake but the goose was in deep slumber. As a ritual a merchant blew a conch shell. Hearing this, the owl made a raucous screech in fear and flew away. This screech being a bad omen, the angry merchants ordered their archer who could hit any source of sound, to kill the miscreant. The archer then threw his arrow targeting the original source of the sound and it killed the goose still asleep in the abode of the owl.

Lessons: i) Bad Company always invites trouble.

12. The Innocent Camel, and the Mischievous Crow, Jackal and Leopard

Sanjivaka to Damanaka

A merchant called Sagardatta, in a business venture, was passing through a forest with 100 camel-drawn caravans loaded with textile articles. By accident one of the camels named Krathanaka buckled under the heavy load of merchandise and was unable to move. As the merchant could not waste time, the load of the broken down caravan was distributed over the other caravans and they continued their journey leaving behind the injured helpless camel. But by good luck Krathanaka came round in a few days and soon became sturdy and went alone roaming hither and thither in the unknown forest. In the meantime, Madatkata, the lion king of that forest, while making a hunting trip inside the forest with his retinues, a crow, a jackal and a leopard, discovered the awkward looking strange animal, the camel. By asking Krathanaka the lion learnt that the latter was a kind of animal called camel. The camel also told the lion and his ministers how he happened to be in this forest which was completely unknown to him. Notwithstanding the intentions of his ministers to kill the camel, the lion felt sympathy for the camel and assured that henceforth he would get the protection of the lion and could move in the forest without fear.

By misfortune, the lion got seriously injured in a fight with a bull elephant. This made him bed ridden and incapable of hunting any animal. His three ministers tried their best but they did not have any capability to hunt animals. In fact, they depended for their food on the leftover of the killed animals after the lion had eaten his part. Thus all of them were at the point of dying of starvation as it was likely to take some time for the lion to get well and be capable of hunting again. The three ministers suggested the lion that for the time being they could arrange for their meals by killing the camel. The lion decline this vile suggestion reminding them that he cannot commit sin by violating his promise to give protection to the camel. Thereafter the three ministers asked the lion that would he kill the camel if he willingly sacrifices his life to save the king from starvation. The lion had no objection to this proposal. Then the three rascals hatched out a nasty plan. They brought the camel along with them to the lion. Then the crow expressed the wish that he would sacrifice his life to save the king from starvation. The other two said that by offering his life the crow had done a pious job. Then the jackal as planned before said that the paltry meat of the crow would be quite inadequate for the meal of the lion. Then he offered to sacrifice his own life to save their king. Everyone praised him for his noble intention. However, the leopard used some ruse to give objection to it and prompted to sacrifice his own life for the king. After praising him the other two ministers used some ruse to give objection to this. Then the camel thought that if he now offers his life he would be praised and like the earlier cases, somebody must give objection to it. So the innocent camel expressed desire to sacrifice his life to save the king from starvation. Nobody, however, objected to the desire of the camel and the lion and his three ministers immediately killed the camel and came out of starvation by devouring his flesh.

Lessons: i) A powerful natural enemy with villainous counselors should never be trusted as a friend.

13. The Lion and the Chariot Maker

Sanjivaka to Damanaka

A chariot maker, called Devagupta, used to fell trees in a forest in order to collect timber for the chariots. He always carried boxes full of curries, sweetmeats and other dainties prepared by his wife for his meal in course of the daylong labour. One day, while engrossed in felling a tree a fierce lion called Vimala appeared at the spot. Devagupta did not find any time to climb up a tree in order to protect his life. As the last endeavour he prayed to the lion to spare his life and meet his hunger by the delicious food in his box. At first the flesh-eater lion was reluctant to eat cooked food in exchange for raw flesh of Devagupta. But the latter could ultimately convince the lion to have a taste of cooked food and sweetmeat prepared by his wife. The taste of the food was so pleasing that the lion was extremely gratified and requested Devagupta to bring such food every day for him. At the request of Devagupta the lion promised that he would not disclose this matter to any third person. Thereafter the lion started eating only the cooked food obtained from Devagupta and gave up hunting animals. This put two hangers on of the lion, a crow and a jackal into trouble as they had to survive on the leftover of the hunted animals by the lion. They tried their best to learn the reason for which the lion had given up hunting. At first the lion kept his promise to Devagupta and declined to disclose anything to the two hangers on. But with continued efforts they could ultimately be successful in learning the matter of Devagupta. The two hangers on conspired to accompany the lion while he goes out to meet Devagupta and then they would somehow provoke the lion to kill the man. This would provide enough food for them and they would be able to gratify their taste of human blood and flesh. With utmost request and oaths that they would do no harm to the man, the lion permitted them to accompany him while he went out to meet Devagupta. Devagupta was waiting for the lion as usual. But that day he found something unusual and ominous. He found a jackal and a crow accompanying the lion. Finding these two animals, well-known for their mischievous characters, with the lion Devagupta apprehended risk of his life. So, he climbed up to a high branch of a nearby tree in time.

Lessons: i) A person with mischievous associates should never be trusted.

14. Uttanapada, the Lapwing who defied the Ocean

Damanaka to Sanjivaka

A lapwing, called Uttanapada, and his wife Pativrata used to live happily in the seashore. When Pativrata was heavy with eggs she entreated her husband to find some safe nook for laying her eggs. She expressed her apprehension that at high tide water of the ocean might enter their abode by accident and destroy the eggs. However, the arrogant and proud Uttanapada declined to leave their abode and out of vanity said that the ocean would not have the audacity to incur enmity with a powerful person like him by sweeping away their eggs. The worried wife tried her best to make her husband come to senses and realise how helpless they were vis-à-vis the overwhelmingly mighty ocean. But Uttanapada was crazy with vanity and adamant to remain in their abode. The wife felt helpless but she could not humiliate her husband by being disobedient. The audacity of the tiny bird made the ocean chuckle and he decided to give him an exemplary lesson. Soon Pativrata laid her eggs but always remained worried about the eggs. One day while the birds were out foraging, the ocean extended some waves as far as the abode of the birds and snatched away the eggs but did not destroy them.

Returning home the birds found that the eggs had been swept away by the ocean. Pativrata started lamenting. But the arrogant and proud Uttanapada started picking up with his small beak water from the ocean declaring that he would take revenge by making the ocean dry. His wife then convinced him that he had undertaken a ridiculous task but it could be done if all the birds make efforts to this end jointly. Now the husband consulted all the birds and the birds went on making concerted efforts to get the ocean dried up by all conceivable means. But soon they realised that this was an impossible task. So, they decided to consult an ancient and wise goose in this regard. The wise goose listened attentively to the sad story of the lapwing family and their burning desire to avenge the mischief of the ocean. The wise goose said that only Lord Garuda, the king of the birds and mount of Lord

Vishnu, has the power to punish the mighty ocean. So, he took all the birds along to Garuda and related to him the story of the tortured lapwings. Hearing this Garuda got angry but he restrained himself from taking any measure on his own. He knew that the ocean was the abode of Lord Vishnu and punishing the ocean would be a humiliation of his lord. So, he reported the matter to his lord telling him that he was much aggrieved at the grave mischief committed by the wicked ocean to one of his subjects. Lord Vishnu paid heed to his mount. Thereafter the Lord warned the ocean that if he did not return the eggs of the lapwings immediately he would make it dry by releasing his fire arrow. Hearing this warning from Lord Vishnu the terrified ocean returned the eggs of the lapwings, apologized to them and promised that in future he would never indulge in any such mischief. Since then the lapwing couple lived in their own abode happily.

Lessons: i) One should not hurt and incur enmity of an apparently weak person without knowing his potential power.

14a. Kambugriva, the Turtle and the Two Geese

Sub Story-1: Pativrata, the wife of Uttanapada to the latter

In a lake lived a turtle named Kambugriva and he had cordial friendship with two geese who used to fish in that lake. Because of a prolonged drought the lake almost got dried up, most of the fishes living there died and so the geese decided to move to a new deeper lake with plenty of water and fishes. When they met the turtle to bid him goodbye, the turtle said that he would also die while the lake gets completely bereft of water. So, he too liked to be transported by the geese to the new lake. The geese told that they would be most happy to do so but the task appeared almost impossible to them. The turtle then advised them that they could carry him by means of a twig. Then the turtle brought a strong twig, held the middle of it firmly with his teeth and asked each goose to hold a side of the stick with his bill. The birds followed this instruction and started carrying the turtle hanging at the middle of the stick. They, however, had cautioned the turtle beforehand that he should never talk on the way because that would make him fall down from the heights and die instantly. The turtle had followed the instructions of the birds for some time. Soon they were passing above a village. The villagers got astonished to find such a strange sight of two birds carrying a turtle by means of a stick. So they started hollering and running on the field following the flight of the birds. All these made the turtle curious and he forgot the good advice of the birds. He suddenly opened his mouth and was about to ask the birds why the people had been hollering and running. But before he could utter anything he fell down on the field to be good food for the people there.

Lessons: i) Ignoring the advice of good friends may lead to disaster.

14b. The Three Fishes – Anagatabidhata, Pratyutpannamati and Yadbhabishya

Sub Story-2: Pativrata, the wife of Uttanapada to the latter

In a lake full of fishes, there lived three large fishes named respectively Anagatabidhata, Pratyutpannamati and Yadbhabishya. As their names suggest the first one of them was always very cautious and if apprehended any danger took prior measures to avert it. The second one true to his name was endowed with keen presence of mind so that he by applying sheer intelligence could come out of predicament that befell him. The third as his name suggests, never cared for the oncoming dangers and always left everything to fate. One day, while basking in the sun, they overheard the talks of some fishermen of a nearby village that the very next day they would set very large nets in the lake and drag out every fish by the nets. They also said that they would see to it that not a single fish is able to escape from their nets. Hearing this Anagatabidhata suggested the other two fishes to escape immediately through the connecting channel to the larger and deeper lake which is inaccessible to the nets of the fishermen. At this Pratyutpannamati opined that he would not at once abandon his old residence but if caught by the nets he would surely apply some trick by means of his presence of mind to fool the fishermen and escape from their grips. Yadbhabishya, however, was happy go lucky and laughed at the advice of the first fish. He said that no one should be overcautious and act according to some rumours about what is going to happen in future. So he ridiculed the first fish and remained carefree. The first fish then left for the deeper lake leaving behind his friends. The next morning true to their announcement the fishermen threw large nets into the lake and all fishes including Pratyutpannamati and Yadbhabishya were caught in the net. Apprehending the danger, Pratyutpannamati by means of his presence of mind feigned to be dead. Finding him already dead the fishermen took him out of the net and kept at a nearby place. The released fish did not lose a single moment to move fast and escape into the water of the lake. Yadbhabishya, on the other hand, made all efforts to break through the net but failed. Then the fishermen hit him with clubs and killed him before taking out of the net.

Lessons: i) One ought not to ignore the good advices of the well-wishers.

14c. The Sparrow and the Crazy Elephant

Sub Story-3: Pativrata, the wife of Uttanapada to the latter

In the leaning branch of a great Tamala tree in a dense forest lived a sparrow couple in a nest happily. One day a crazy elephant under the spell of spring fever happened to take shelter in the shade of the tree. Spring fever had made the elephant restless and in utter excitement he dragged at the branch containing the nest of the sparrows. The two birds could escape in time but their nest was crashed and all their offsprings killed. While the sparrows were lamenting piteously at the loss of their abode and children, their best friend, a woodpecker, came forward. Inspecting about the reason for their lamentation, the woodpecker said that it was no use pining over what had been lost. It would be better to find out some means to punish the mischievous elephant. He also said that a weak person alone may not match a strong enemy, but if united with similar weak persons he could outmatch the stronger enemy by means of their combined power. So he took the sparrow family to another friend, a gnat called Vinarava. Hearing the mischief of the elephant and the resolve of the sparrows to punish the miscreant he again took them to another friend, a frog called Meghaduta. Now, the four friends conferred and devised a full proof plan to punish the elephant. According to the plan the gnat Vinarava started humming around the ears of the elephant a very sweet and love inspiring song. At this the crazy elephant infected with spring fever closed his eyes and started enjoying the melodious song. At this very moment, as arranged, the woodpecker, with his sharp beak injured seriously the eyes of the elephant making him completely blind. Then the elephant, in severe pain of the damaged and bleeding eyes, started running frantically in circles around the area. Soon he became thirsty and was looking out frantically for drinking water. As the group of friends could realise from the movements of the elephant that he was looking for water, the frog, seated at the corner of a stiff ditch started croaking loudly. The croaking of the frog made the elephant believe that there must be water at the source of the croaking, which is very usual, he ran towards the ditch very fast to quench his indomitable thirst. He soon reached the ditch, fell into it and died instantly. Thus being united, four weak friends could punish the mighty elephant for his mischief perpetrated on the poor sparrows.

Lessons: i) Unity is strength. Weak persons, if united, can overpower a strong enemy.

14d. The Ancient Wild Goose and the Fowler

Sub Story-4: An Intelligent Bird to Uttanapada and Other Birds

In certain forest there was a massive banyan tree. On its spread out branches lived a large number of wild geese. Once the wisest of the birds observed a creeper called Kosambi climbing up the banyan tree. He apprehended that soon this plant would reach the branches of the tree making it accessible for hunters to climb up the then inaccessible tree. As the old bird was weak due to age and was unable to destroy the creeper himself, he warned the other geese about the impending danger of the rising creeper and requested them to nip in the bud the foreseeable disaster by uprooting the creeper without wasting any time. But the other geese did not pay heed to the warning of the wise old goose. On the contrary they ridiculed the old bird for his overcautious nature. As the wise goose had apprehended, the creeper soon reached the branches of the banyan tree. One day, while all the geese were out foraging, a group of hunters climbed the three with the help of the creeper and laid bird catching traps on all the branches of the tree. The old bird was at home and at the approach of the hunters he escaped to a distant tree. In the evening the geese returned to the tree and were all caught unawares in the bird catching nets. The wild goose returning home at night found the predicament of the fellow geese, a punishment for disregarding his good advice. But now it was his duty to find some means to set the fellow geese free instead of reprimanding them for their foolishness. He advised all the geese to pretend to be dead while the hunters would come the next morning to collect the birds caught.

Next morning the hunters climbed up the tree and finding the birds already dead, started releasing them from the nets one by one and throwing down on the ground. When the last bird had been released the wise goose gave a signal and all the geese rose and simultaneously flew away out of the reach of the hunters.

Lessons: i) Ancient people are likely to be wise and possessing experience. And so it is always beneficial to respect them and pay heed to their advices.

14e. The Lion and the Lone Ram

Sub-story-5: The Ancient Wild Goose to Garuda, the king of the birds

Once a plump and woolly lamb happened to stray away from its group and lost its way in the forest. He started groping around with a view to finding out an escape route from the forest so as to get united again with his group. In the meantime a lion while looking for animals to be hunted saw the lamb, an awkward strange animal looking very fierce. The sight of the ram made the lion frightened and in order to find out what king of animal it was, the lion took shelter in a bush and started observing the movements of the lone ram. After long random movement the ram felt hungry and began to graze the lush grasses grown in an open space inside the forest. Observing this the lion could realize that the ram was but a grass eating animal, a prey for clawed animals like a lion. He felt ashamed of his earlier fear for such an animal and ran very fast towards the ram and before the latter could escape, jumped on him and killed him.

Lessons: i) Weak persons ought not to disclose to the stronger natural enemies the activities that may identify their weaknesses and vulnerabilities. They should indulge in such activities in secret, out of the sight of the natural enemies.

15. The Cunning Jackal and the Foolish Lion

Damanaka to Karataka

A female camel from a nearby village used to graze in a field close to a forest. In the forest lived a lion called Vazradangsta with his attendant called Chaturaka, a very cunning jackal. The jackal could not hunt any animal by his own capabilities and therefore he had to depend for food on the left over after the lion had eaten any animal hunted by him. Chaturaka was extremely selfish and did not hesitate to undertake any unethical activity that could serve his self-interest. One day while the jackal was moving alone at the border of the forest he got the glimpse of the grazing camel. He thought that if this camel could be tempted somehow to get inside the forest and get killed by his lord they would have sumptuous food for some time. With this vile intention in mind he made friendship with the innocent camel. Thereafter he informed the lion about the lucrative plump camel and requested him to keep him in hiding in a bush. The lion followed the directions of the jackal and remained hidden in a nearby bush. The jackal then met the camel and in course of gossips brought the latter close to the bush where the lion was in ambush. The lion did not hesitate to kill the helpless camel.

In the meantime, merchants with camel drawn caravans were moving along the high road by the forest. The bells hanging from the necks of the camels were making jingling sounds which with multiple echoes appeared horrible to the lion who ordered Chaturaka to inspect the source of the sound. Getting closer to the road he observed that the source of the sound. At that moment he had a mischievous idea. He thought that if he could frighten away the lion by making some story about the procession of the merchants he would be able to feed on the dead camel for a long time. Returning to the lion the jackal with seemingly panic stricken eyes said that it was a procession of the ancestors of the dead camel with gods and he had heard them talking that they would kill the lion for committing the grave crime of killing a female camel. Hearing this, the lion flee away to a distant place never to return again and the cunning jackal got the opportunity of eating on the flesh of the big camel for a long time.

Lessons: i) A conscienceless cunning person is concerned with his own interest alone and in order to serve his vile purpose can always device means to deceive others.

16. King Suratha, Minister Balabhadra and the Naked Mendicant

Karataka to Damanaka

King Suratha of the kingdom of Kosala had a very honest minister and he possessed deep political wisdom. Besides expertise in diplomacy he was also a very good war strategist. Once a forest chieftain named Vindhyaka rose in revolt against king Suratha. In order to punish the miscreant the king sent minister Balabhadra with his soldiers.to the forest Taking advantage of the absence of the wise minister a naked mendicant suddenly made his appearance in Ayadhya, the capital of the Kosala kingdom. With his knowledge of astrology and Atharva Vedic practices the mendicant soon became popular among the residents of the city and many of the people of the city became his disciples. Soon he could make his way into the royal court and by means of his magic practices he soon won the heart of the king. The enchanted king started believing in the divine power of the mendicant. The mendicant used to come to the court of the king and after showing off of his magic feats left with lucrative rewards from the king. One day the mendicant was absent and when he came the next day the king asked him about the reason of his absence. At this the mendicant said that he in meditation had left his coarse body and in fine body had visited the heaven and all the gods there. He said that he had also met the ancestors of the king who had asked him about the well-being of the king. So, he got a greater reward from the king that day. The next day the minister Balabhadra returned after the successful mission of punishing the miscreant. As he learnt about the mendicant from the king and other city dwellers, he, by means of his acute intelligence, could realise that the mendicant was but a swindler. So he decided to teach him a good lesson. The next day when the mendicant came to the royal court the minister requested him to visit heaven again and meet the ancestors of the minister. Balabhadra promised a sumptuous reward to the mendicant if the latter could gather information of his ancestors from heaven. The greedy mendicant said that he would soon do so and took the minister and the king close to his cottage. Before entering the cottage he told the minister that he would travel in fine body to heaven right after shutting the door of the cottage and return after two hours with all information of the ancestors of the minister. As soon as the mendicant shut the door of the cottage Balabhadra sought permission of the king to set fire on the cottage of the mendicant. He explained to the bamboozled king that if the coarse body of the mendicant is burnt then only his fine heavenly body would remain. So, thereafter, the king, the minister and all the citizens of the country would have the good fortune of encountering a heavenly mendicant forever. With the permission of king Suratha, Balabhadra got the hut of the fake mendicant set on fire burning alive the mendicant and making the city free from the deceptive practices of the fake mendicant.

Lessons: i) A minister with wisdom of statecraft and diplomacy is one of the greatest assets of a king.

16a. The Maiden and Her Snake Husband

Sub Story: Balabhadra to King Suratha

A Brahmana called Deva Sharma lived with his wife in the city of Rajagriha. They were unhappy as they did not have any children. At last Deva Sharma met a pious ascetic and prayed to him with deep devotion asking for a son. The ascetic was pleased at the prayer of the king and blessed him that soon his wife would give birth to a very auspicious son. Unfortunately the Brahmani, instead of delivering a son, gave birth to a male snake. Disregarding the advices of the neighbours to abandon the snake child, the Brahmani reared him with utmost care of a mother. When the snake was grown up and achieved the age of marriage, the Brahmani requested her husband to find a suitable bride to be married with her son. At first Deva Sharma tried to convince his wife that none would be willing to offer a daughter for marriage with a snake. But as the Brahmani was very adamant, Deva Sharma left home in quest of a bride for his snake son. After long travel he at last came to a village where the host in whose house Deva Sharma was accepted as a guest, was also a Brahmana. Soon he became a good friend of Deva Sharma and asked him the purpose of his travel. Deva Sharma said that he had been looking for a bride for his grown up son. The host Brahmana had been very much impressed by the physical features and civilized behaviour of Deva Sharma. He thought that the son of such a person must be handsome and educated like his father. So, without making any further enquiry about the son of Deva Sharma, he proposed to offer his grown up daughter to marriage with the son of the latter. According to custom of the country, the daughter with some relatives accompanied Deva Sharma to Rajagriha for marriage with the groom. However, as soon as they arrived near the house of Deva Sharma, his neighbours disclosed to the relatives of the bride that the prospective groom was but a snake. Learning this, the relatives of the bride decided to cancel the marriage and return immediately with the bride. But the bride prevented them from doing so. She said that her father had already offered her for marriage to the son of Deva Sharma, and a daughter cannot be offered for marriage twice and words given cannot be violated. So she compelled them to get her married with the snake.

In the bridal night she was surprised to find a beautiful young man coming out of the shell of the snake, the shell remaining at the corner of the door. She enjoyed the bridal night and her husband once again entered into the snake shell at the close of the night. Next day she informed her in-laws of her experience. Then she hatched out a plan with her in laws. That night she kept the doors ajar, and as soon as the husband came out of the snake shell, Deva Sharma entered the room and set the snake shell on fire. Thereafter the couple lived happily and Deva Sharma, his wife and all the neighbours were happy at the incidence of the snake turning into a handsome young man.

Lessons: i) Word given should not be returned.

ii) One ought to inquire thoroughly about the groom/bride before promising to offer his daughter/son to marriage.

16a-1: Death and Indra's Parrot

Chain Story: The Maiden to her relations

Indra, the king of the gods, had a very beautiful parrot which was dear to all the gods of heaven. She had a charming singing voice and she could also chant Vedic verses correctly. One day, while Yama, the god controlling death was about to enter the court of Indra in order to pay the routine respect to his king, the parrot immediately escaped and hid herself behind a wall. While the gods asked the reason for her unusual behaviour, the parrot replied that she was afraid that Yama, the god controlling death had come to take her life. Indra and all the other gods then requested Yama not to take the life of this beautiful bird. At this Yama said that he has no power over ones death, he takes the soul only when Time orders him to do so, i.e. the time of one's death approaches. The gods then met Time and at their request of sparing the life of the parrot he said that actual decision about this is taken by Death himself. Thereafter the gods proceeded to the house of Death but at the sheer sight of Death, the parrot fell dead. While asked about the incident, Yama explained that it had been pre-ordained that the parrot would die at the mere sight of Death. It was her destiny and nobody can alter his destiny.

Lessons: i) None can reverse his destiny.

17. The Tailor Bird and the Ape

Karataka to Damanaka

In a forest there lived a troop of silly monkeys. It was very cold the in that winter and in the evening the monkeys were shivering in cold. Suddenly the apes found a firefly that was flying around the place. A monkey caught it and all the monkeys thought it to be a source of fire. So they piled up dried leafs and logs around the insect and started to get their body warmed up by imagining the insect to be real fire. With increase in coldness the hardship of the monkeys went on increasing. Still they, out of folly, tried to get heat from the firefly. In the meantime a tailor-bird observed their folly and trying to get them convinced that that the thing they thought of as fire is but a firefly having no power to provide heat. But the silly monkeys went on ignoring the suggestions of the bird and started becoming angry with the bird. The bird in order to convince them got closer to the apes to show them what the seeming source of fire really was. Increasing bite of coldness had already made the apes crazy. So as soon as the tiny bird came closer to them, one of the monkeys caught hold of her and crashed her to death.

Lessons: i) Nobody can teach a person who is determined not to learn.

18. Dharmabuddhi and Dustabuddhi

Karataka to Damanaka

Two friends Dharmabuddhi (Ethical Person) and Dustabuddhi (Wicked Person) consulted to travel in quest of fortune as all their painstaking endeavours at the native place had produced no results. As the names suggest, the first friend was very honest and ethical but the second one, unethical and wicked. They travelled many villages, found some trifling works, but could not earn the fortune they had expected to. In this way they entered into a forest and close to an abandoned dilapidated mansion they found a mound. Expecting treasure inside it they started digging the mound and lo, they came upon a safe full of gold coins. Dharmabuddhi proposed that they should now return home dividing the treasure equally between the two friends. At this Dustabuddhi said that it would not be safe to take so much wealth to their houses. So it would be better to take hundred coins each and hide the rest in some safe place. After they had spent these hundred coins they would again take hundred coins more and so on. Dharmabuddhi agreed to the proposal which appeared logical to him. Accordingly, after taking out hundred coins each the two friends hid the safe in a pit under a tree in the forest. They marked the tree with a sign so that it could be recognised later on. Returning home the wicket friend thought of stealing the rest of the gold coins stored in the safe. So after a few days he went to the hiding spot, dug out the safe and left home with it and hid it underground in the courtyard of his house. After both had spent the initial hundred coins Dustabuddhi proposed to his friend that it was now time to take out the second installment of hundred coins each. But digging the hiding spot they found nothing and Dustabuddhi alleged that the safe had been stolen by Dharmabuddhi. They quarreled on this issue and at last Dustabuddhi complained to the court of the king against his friend for stealing the hidden wealth. To confirm his allegations Dustabuddhi suggested taking evidence of a tree close to the spot of the hiding place of the treasure. The judges could not believe that a tree could give evidence like human beings. But Dustabuddhi said that he had seen such a tree and requested the judges to test the truthfulness of his opinion. The judges got amazed at this but out of curiosity they agreed to examine next morning the validity of the opinion of Dustabuddhi. Returning home Dustabuddhi, after much endeavour, could make his reluctant father agree to hide inside a big hole at the trunk of the tree which Dustabuddhi had chosen as the witness and give false evidence next morning that Dharmabuddhi had stolen the treasure. Next morning, when the judges sought evidence of the tree as regards stealing of the treasure, the father of Dustabuddhi, from the crevice of the tree, said in a queer voice that it was Dharmabuddhi who had stolen the entire wealth. At this the judges decided to punish Dharmabuddhi. But the latter, realising the mystery, promptly gathered dried leaves around the trunk of the tree and set fire on them. The smoke from the fire reached the hole where the imposter father of Dustabuddhi had been hiding, and in panic he came out and confessed the guilt of himself and his son. On the basis of their confession the treasure could be recovered by digging out the courtyard of Dustabuddhi. He along with his father was sent to prison and Dharmabuddhi, absolved of all allegations, was rewarded by the judges with the entire treasure.

Lessons: i) Crime does not pay. A criminal son may incriminate even his parents.

18a. The Foolish Heron

Sub Story: Father of Dustabuddhi to the Latter

In a vast banyan tree lived a large number of herons. Suddenly a serpent came from somewhere and took shelter in a hole of the tree. Soon the vehement snake started devouring the offsprings of the herons. But the weak herons could not do anything against the powerful enemy in order to protect their offsprings. One of the herons with much grief because of loss of his children went to the side of the lake and started weeping. A crab living in the lake was surprised to find the heron, who at this hour should have been busy catching fish, weeping with downcast head. The crab with great curiosity got closer to the bank of the lake and asked the heron the reason for his sorrow. At the query of the crab the heron disclosed in detail the misfortune of the herons because of the mischievous serpent. Hearing this it appeared to the mind of the crab that this vulnerable condition of the herons, his natural enemies, could be taken advantage of to destroy them. So the crab expressed sympathy with the herons and said that he could suggest a means to punish the serpent. He pointed out to the heron that a mongoose, the natural enemy of the snakes, lives in a burrow close to the tree. If the herons scatter pieces of fish right from the burrow of the mongoose up to the hollow of the serpent in the tree the mongoose, following the trails of the pieces of fish would reach the serpent hole and kill him.

The heron thanked the crab for his good advice and soon informed of this remedy to other herons. Thereafter all the herons started picking up pieces of fish and scattering them from the mouth of the burrow of the mongoose up to the abode of the snake on the tree. The mongoose as expected followed the trail of the pieces of fish and soon reached the abode of the snake on the tree and killed him. But this also gave him access to the nests of the herons. Gradually the mongoose started killing and devouring the herons from their nests and in course of time all the foolish herons were exterminated as expected by the shrewd crab.

Lessons: i) No one should depend on the advice of a natural enemy as it may ultimately lead to his own disaster.

19. Jirnadhana, the Merchant and the Swindler Seth

Karataka to Damanaka

Jirnadhana, the son of a merchant was in a precarious condition after business failure. Being unable to restore his position in the locality, he decided to try his luck in some distant region. To this end he borrowed money from Lakshmana, the Seth (chief of the merchants' guild). As a pledge he deposited with his ancestral balance made of hundred kilos of iron.

Fortunately he was successful in business in foreign land and after earning adequate amount of money he decided to return to his native city. Returning home he first met Lakshmana and repaid his lone. But while asked for the balance he had deposited the Seth said that it had been devoured by rats. Jirnadhana left without protesting against this conspicuous lie as he had something else in his mind. He was determined to give the unscrupulous merchant a good lesson and soon he got a golden opportunity to get his desire fulfilled. One day while going to the market he came upon the son of Lakshmana near their house and said that he was feeling ill. So it would be of much help to him if the son could accompany him to the market. Lakshmana did not object to this proposal and permitted his son to accompany Jirnadhana. Instead of going to the market Jirnadhana took the son of Lakshmana to a dilapidated house and tied him inside a room with a rope, closing his mouth with some cloth so that he could not make any noise. Soon Jirnadhana returned and told Lakshmana that his son had been snatched away by a hawk. This made Lakshmana furious and he immediately complained to the king. The Royal judges asked Jirnadhana how it could be possible for a hawk to carry away a young boy. Jirnadhana replied calmly that this is possible if it is possible for rats to eat away an iron balance. Then he told the judges the story from the beginning. Thereafter at the request of the judges he returned Lakshmana's son in exchange for his balance. The judges punished Lakshmana with a heavy fine for his mischief.

Lesson: i) An unscrupulous person is accustomed to indulging in blatant lies in order to get his vile design fulfilled.

20. The Two Similar Parrots and the Prince

Karataka to Damanaka

In a tree near a mountain there were two parrot offsprings who looked exactly alike. Their parents used to go out foraging everyday keeping the chics in the nest. One day, in the absence of their parents, a fowler chief caught the two chics from their nest and decided to rear them as pets. On the way, however, one of the chics could manage to escape and after flying some distance he got asylum in the cottage of a good hermit. Thereafter, both of the chics were brought up with care and taught to talk but in different milieus.

After few years a prince was going along with his entourage to visit a friend. On the way his horse got panicked at the sight of a snake and strayed away into the forest. The horse lost its way and started moving randomly. Soon the horse with the prince got close to the village of the fowlers and the parrot reared by the chief of the fowlers found the prince on horseback approaching. Then the bird started hollering, "My lord, here comes on horseback a man with jewellery. Please come, kill him and loot his horse and jewellery". Hearing this, the frightened prince spurred his horse hard to move away fast from the place. After some time they got close to the cottage of the hermit. Observing the horse mounted prince the other bird from the cage said politely, "Oh, revered prince, get down and take rest in our cottage." Then addressing the hermit he said, "Guruji, a noble prince has come to our cottage. He is very tired after long journey. Please arrange for his proper reception as an honourable guest." Listening to completely opposite things from two similar birds the prince got extremely surprised. He immediately got down from horseback and told this bird about his experience with a similar looking bird in the village of the fowlers. In response to the query of the prince the bird told him the story since their childhood. He also explained that he and his brother have diametrically opposite behaviour because of upbringing in two opposite cultural milieus.

Lessons: i) The character of a person depends a good deal on the cultural milieu in which he is brought up.

21. The Noble Foe and Faithful but Foolish Friend

Karataka to Damanaka

a) The Noble Foe

A prince had deep friendship with the son of a merchant and that of a scholar. They spent their time gossiping, playing games and indulging in various other forms of merry making. They never had any liking for education and in the professions of their parents. Because of this wayward behaviour all the three friends had been regularly reprimanded by their parents. This unending scolding from their families appeared unendurable to them and they decided to leave home. They also took a vow that they would not return home unless they could earn wealth and education. They went on passing through many towns and villages. One day outside a village they found a cottage where they came upon a rishi like man with long beard and bright eyes. They offered pronam to the sage and requested him to make them his disciples and impart them education. At this the sage smiled and said, "Of course I would help you get educated. But education is meaningless without wealth. So at first earn wealth. In fact I can tell you how you could be rich. In fact I was the son of a very rich person. But I preferred a spiritual life. So I sold all inherited wealth, purchased three invaluable gems with them and hid them in a cave shut by a magic stone. I expected that the gems should fall in some good hands. Now I realise that you are the right persons to own the gems. I would give you direction of the cave, teach you the mantra to remove the stone lid of the cave and also the mantra that would enable you to hide the gems in your stomach for security and take them out again when necessary." Learning the mantras and getting the direction of the cave from the sage, the three friends proceeded for the cave. In two days' arduous journey through dense forest they could ultimately discover the cave. Uttering the mantra they opened the cave and came out with the invaluable gems. They soon gulped the gems with the help of the mantra taught by the hermit. A robber who had heard about the gems had been trying hard for some time but failed to remove the stone from the mouth of the cave. Now from a hiding place he observed the three friends obtaining and gulping the gems. He decided to accompany them and kill them unawares at some secret place, split open their bellies and get possession of the gems.

He approached the three friends saying that he had lost way in the forest and was frightened being alone. It would be helpful if they permit him to accompany them and get out of the forest safe. The three friends agreed to take him along. Soon evening fell and before the robber could attack and kill the three friends a band of Bhils, a ferocious forest tribe, caught them and took them to their village. A pet parrot of the Bhil-chieftain declared in bird-language that the captives had valuable gems with them.

Depending on the statement of the bird the Bhil-chieftain searched the four captives again and again, even making them completely nude. But he got nothing from them. But still the bird went on declaring that they possess valuable gems. According to experience of the chieftain the bird had never lied. So he thought that the gems might be hidden inside the belly of the captives. According to tribal custom they never killed any human being at night. So he decided to open the bellies of the captives the next dawn in order to search for the gems. Thereafter the captives were shut for the night in a dungeon. At night the robber started reflecting that if the Bhils kill and open the belly of any one of the three friends, they would get gems and they would also open his belly. So under no circumstances his life could be saved. But by sacrificing his life first it might be possible to save the lives of the three friends. This would be a noble death. Thereby he might acquire some virtue that would lighten the weight of the sins he had committed so far. If he forwards himself to be slayed first the Bhils would find nothing in his belly. So they may set the others free thinking that none have any gem inside his belly. Next morning when they were taken to the killing ground, the robber fell on the feet of the Bhil chieftain and said that he would not be able to endure the death of his friends. So he would be thankful to the chieftain if he was killed first sparing him from viewing the killings of his dear friends. The chieftain was moved by the entreaty of the robber. But opening his belly and splitting other limbs he found no gem anywhere. This filled the minds of the chieftain and his followers with a sense of guilt for killing an innocent person for no reason at all. He thought that he might have made some mistake this time in reading the language of the bird. So to avoid further sin he released the prince and his friends. Thereafter the three friends proceeded for the Ashrama for having the necessary education from the great sage. Their hearts were filled with utmost gratitude for the stranger (the robber) for his exemplary sacrifice.

b) The Foolish Friend

A king had a very favourite monkey. He was very strong, of pleasant behaviour and had learnt the art of using swords very efficiently. So the king honoured the monkey with the positions of the guard of his bed room and his bodyguard. The monkey was very obedient to the king, the queen, the ministers, princes and all others in the court of the king. Everybody in the kingdom loved the monkey and the king himself considered the ape to be his best friend. One day the king felt very tired and sleepy at noon because of heavy activities since morning. He felt the necessity of sound sleep without being disturbed by anybody. So he instructed the monkey to guard the room and allow nobody to disturb him during his sleep. Thereafter the king relapsed into deep slumber. Suddenly a housefly entered through the crevice of a window and sat on an arm of the king. The monkey with the motion of his hand drove the fly away. But the fly again sat on the chest of the king. The monkey did his best to make the fly refrain from disturbing the king, but the adamant fly went on disturbing the king by sitting on this or that part of the body of the king. Ultimately the monkey got horribly angry and drew out his sword. At that time the fly was seated by the side of the neck of the sleeping king. The foolish monkey attempted to kill the fly by hitting it with the sword and the king was beheaded and killed at once. The noise made by the sword made everybody rush into the room. To their horror they found the king beheaded by the act of the silly monkey. So they killed the foolish monkey in no time.

Lessons: i) A noble foe is better than a foolish friend.

Chapter-3: Tantra II-Pilgrimage for Friendship

Primary Story: Pilgrimage of the Crow Laghupatanaka for Friendship

This tantra pertains to the pilgrimage of the crow named Laghupatanaka for friendship. The mission came to fruition with the participation of three more agents – a mouse named Hiranyaka, a tortoise named Mantharaka and a deer named Chitranga. The pilgrimage that went through many hazards had its culmination in the glorious achievement of an unbreakable and noble bond of friendship among four physically resource-less and apparently powerless agents from diverse classes of animals – the crow, a bird; the mouse, a rodent; the tortoise, an aquatic animal and a deer, a grass eating mammal. Although they apparently lacked resources, they had mental resources of wisdom, fellow feeling, indefatigable resolve and noble intentions.

The incident that inspired the crow to venture into this pilgrimage is as follows.

In southern part of India there was a city called Mahilaropya. At the outskirts of the city was a gigantic banyan tree that gave shelter to a host of variegated birds, insects, reptiles and the vast umbrella of its shadow was the resting place of many other animals.

In this tree lived the crow Laghupatanaka of our story. One day while seated on another nearby tree, he found a horrible looking fowler approaching the banyan tree. Soon the devil opened a vast net with bird catching meshes and spread it close to the banyan tree. As baits to tempt the victims, he spread grain seeds on the net. Realizing his evil intentions, the crow soon informed all the birds and cautioned them about the danger behind the lucrative grains. Before he could fully caution the king of the dove Chitragriva, the latter, along with the entire dove entourage dropped on the net lured by the grains and was caught with his entourage in the meshes of the net. Chitragriva, however, did not lose head under this grave predicament which came all of a sudden like a bolt from the blue. Like a true leader, he remained cool and through deep thinking devised a probable way out. He ordered his entire retinue to remain united and make a simultaneous effort to fly up with the net. To convince them about the strength of unity and weakness of discord he told the story of the Bharunda Birds. Thereafter the other doves agreed to the proposal and as soon as they found the fowler approaching the net with a large club in his hand they flew together lifting the net high and beyond the reach of the fowler. At this unprecedented incident the fowler got puzzled. He got worried over losing not only the birds caught but also the net, the source of his livelihood. The doves started flying along with the net and expecting that sometimes the birds might get tired or lose unified action, the desperate fowler started running following the flight of the doves. Now following Chitragriva's direction the doves started flying above difficult terrains so that the fowler was compelled to abandon chasing the birds and he returned home in a depressed and dejected heart. Now Chitragriva told the birds to follow a path that would lead them to a place where a mouse called Hiranyaka, a friend of Chitranga, lived and it was quite likely that the mouse would be able to cut off the net and set them all free. The crow Laghupatanaka had got much interested to see what ultimately would happen to the entrapped doves. So he followed the doves flying with the net. Soon the doves landed with the net at a lonely place. Then as Chitragriva called aloud "Hiranyaka", a mouse peeped out from its burrow and finding his friend was very happy and at the same time expressed worry by seeing the condition of his friend and his retinue. At the request of his friend Hiranyaka assured that it was but a simple task for him to set them free. Then he started gnawing at the meshes of the net and soon all the entrapped doves were free and they soon flew towards home. In course of cutting the net the mouse had discoursed on many topics that gave testimony to his wisdom.

The intelligent talks and helpful attitude of the mouse made the crow crazy for having friendship with him. So, after the doves had left he called the mouse and expressed his desire for having friendship with the latter. And here was the beginning of the pilgrimage of the crow for friendship. But the task was a very difficult one for the crow to convince the mouse that the crow, a natural enemy of a mouse who is his food, did not have any evil intention in his mind. As soon as the crow offered the proposal for friendship, there was outright rejection from the mouse. But the crow was determined and was never in a mood to give up. So talks and debates ensued between the two. The oaths made by the crow were not taken seriously by the mouse who clearly said that it was but an evil trick by his natural enemy to fool him. The way the crow talked made Hiranyaka realize in course of time that the crow was intelligent and he might not have evil intensions in his offer of friendship. But still he could not take risk. Ultimately the crow expressed his resolve that unless he was accepted as a friend by the mouse he would remain seated in the tree and die of starvation. The earlier talks and this threat of suicide by the crow at last made the mouse accept the offer of friendship. Then the crow came down from the tree and the mouse came out of its burrow, and they embraced each other as the mark of beginning of the pilgrimage for friendship. Thereafter the crow went out foraging and returned with a piece of flesh of a dead buffalo and offered it to Hiranyaka. The latter too returned with grains he had saved for the crow. In this manner the friendship between the two became deeper and enjoyable through exchange of foods, friendly talks, discussions on various serious topics and embraces. Sometimes the crow flied high with the mouse on his back and at times the mouse slept in the warmth of the feather of the crow. One thing, however, appeared mysterious to the crow. The mouse always looked morose as though disinterested in the matters of this mundane world. But he, out of decency, never expressed curiosity about the personal matters of the mouse.

Unfortunately, because of continued lack of rains, the entire area was affected with severe drought. It was difficult for the crow to collect food as the householders themselves were starving for lack of grains. Moreover, in order to collect food, people were killing the birds that happened to come their way. Thus it was also unsafe for the crow to stay in that place. So, he decided to leave that place and fly to a distant lake where his tortoise friend named Mantharaka lived. The place was safe and endowed with plenty of food for birds and other animals.

The crow with a heavy heart told the mouse all this and regretted that he would have to bid goodbye to a wise and noble friend like Hiranyaka. Hearing all these, the mouse expressed his desire to accompany the crow to the new place. Soon, he too would have to starve as a consequence of the drought. Moreover, for some reason he had become pessimistic and disinterested in worldly matters. A change of place might give him some solace. While the crow asked about the reason for his pessimism, the mouse said that he would give detail of his sad story after moving on to the new place. As regards the problem of transport to the distant place the mouse suggested that the crow might fly with him on the back. The crow liked the proposal. He then described the eight kinds of flying he had been accustomed to, and decided to carry the mouse on his back in 'Easy-even flight' mode which would be safe and comfortable for Hiranyaka.

Thereafter, the crow carried the mouse piggyback and after some time they arrived at the desired place. The crow got settled on a tree by the lake and getting down from his back the mouse took shelter in a crevice of a branch of the tree. Now the crow called aloud the name of the tortoise. Hearing this Slowcoach came out of water and was elated to find Laghupatanaka. The crow and the mouse got down from the tree and got close to the tortoise. The crow introduced the mouse to the tortoise. The tortoise and the mouse gladly accepted each other as friends. After exchange of personal information, all of them took food as arranged by Slowcoach and took some rest. After rest, as promised by Hiranyaka, he started telling his sad story. In brief, the mouse possessed ancestrally a hoard of wealth inside a satchel. Sleeping on this wealth gave him extraordinary power and this had also made him the leader of all the mice living in the fort-like burrow with hundred openings. By dint of his power emanating from the flavour of wealth, he used to loot the alms from the alms-bowl of a mendicant Brahmana. This used to deprive the Brahmana of the food saved for his attendants and enabled Hiranyaka to feed himself and all his followers. Wealth gave him the power to jump very high and move extremely fast. So the Brahmana could by no means protect foods offered by householders in his alms-bowl. But the things changed soon. A guest came to the monastery and after learning about the special power of the mouse, the intelligent Brahmana thought that there ought to be some source of unprecedented power of the mouse. Because of folly of some mice injured by attack of a cat, the Brahmanas could find out a mouth of the burrow. By pickaxe they dug the burrow and discovered the hoard of wealth, the source of uncanny capabilities of Hiranyaka. They then took out the hoard of wealth. With the loss of wealth Hiranyaka lost all power emanating from wealth, his power to jump high and move fast. So he was no longer capable of reaching the alms-bowl high up on the wall of the monastery and unable to provide delicious food to his followers. All the mice now rejected the leadership of penniless Hiranyaka and abandoned him. So, he got extremely depressed and lost interest in worldly matters. At this very moment the entrapped doves came for his help and thereafter Laghupatanaka approached him for friendship. Friendship of the crow had given him some solace. But he had to part with his birth place.

Hearing all these, Slowcoach endeavoured to convince Hiranyaka by means of philosophical discussions. He could ultimately convince Hiranyaka that he should not pine over leaving his birth place because any place a person gets settled in becomes his own in course of time. He also explained that wealth is transitory and to explain this told the story of Samilak, the weaver. Slowcoach explained why friendship and determination are more important than transitory wealth. If one has good friends and strong determination, he can easily achieve wealth and other means of happiness.

Now the mouse was fully convinced that he had lost power of wealth but had achieved something more important and significant, viz. the power of true friendship. Thus the bondage of friendship of the three took them to a higher plane of the pilgrimage for friendship. Soon the group was strengthened by a new friend, a deer called Chitranga.

One day while the three friends were busy conversing, sudden sounds of approaching footsteps made them cautious. They all soon took shelter at safe places. The crow from the branch of a tree found that it was but a tired and thirsty deer approaching the lake for drinking. The three friends then got close to the deer who told that he had to move on day in and day out for fear of hunters. The three friends assured that he could stay at this place free from the menace of hunters. The deer thanked them, mentioned his name as Chitranga and learning about their friendship requested to accept him too in their group. At this the three friends objected by saying that why a large animal like Chitranga would desire to strike up friendship with small animals like them. Then Chitranga said that even small animals can be of help to large animals. To explain this he told them the story of the mice that had rescued the entrapped elephants.

Within a few days the deer also became a close friend of the crow, the mouse and the tortoise. Now the pilgrimage for friendship was complete with four friends from different categories of animals but having the same sort of wisdom and fellow feeling – the Crow, a bird; the Mouse, a rodent; the Tortoise, an aquatic anima; and the Deer, a grass eating mammal. Their friendship got deeper and deeper in course of time. However, the Deer and thereafter the Tortoise had got into some trouble, being caught by a hunter. But by intelligence and efforts of the other friends they could soon come out of the hazards. Thereafter the four friends went on spending time by gossiping, playing, sharing food, and discussing serious matters like economics, politics, philosophy, mythology etc.

Lessons: i) True Friendship is more powerful than transitory material resources like wealth.

ii) Friendship can be struck up among any persons irrespective of their class, creed, category etc. The necessary things for true friendship are wisdom, fellow feeling, honesty and noble intentions.

Secondary Stories
22. Bharunda Birds

Chitragriva, king of the doves to the other ensnared doves

Bharundas are a peculiar kind of birds with one body and two necks. Once, a bharunda bird was foraging. Suddenly one of the necks found a very delicious fruit and picked it up with its beak. The other neck saw this and earnestly requested the lucky neck to give him a share. However out of selfishness the lucky neck denied the request. This made the other neck extremely aggrieved and determined to take revenge. The opportunity came soon. While foraging a few days later, the other neck found a poisonous fruit and to take revenge it soon ate the poisonous fruit. Then the bird with two necks died instantly.

Lessons: i) Persons with common interest should always cooperate with one another. Jealousy and rivalry in such a case may bring about disaster as in the case of the bharunda birds.

23. Causes of Sorrows of Hiranyaka and the Power of Wealth

Hiranyaka, the mouse to Laghupatanaka, the crow and Mantharaka, the tortoise

The burrow of Hiranyaka, near a south Indian city called Promadaropya, was like a fort. It had hundred openings so that there were several escape routes if attacked by enemies. Many other mice lived inside this fort and were followers of Hiranyaka because he had wealth and he was the provider of their food to all of them. Not far from the burrow of Hiranyaka there was a monastery owned by a mendicant monk named Butakarna. Every day the monk with his alms bowl used to make a round of the city and his bowl was filled with delicious food items by the householders. Returning to the monastery he used to take his part from the bowl and preserved the rest in the bowl to be distributed next morning to the attendants. He therefore hanged the bowl with the rest of the food items in a peg high up on the wall of the monastery. But unfortunately the bowl soon became empty as Hiranyaka could always get access to the food bowl and loot the food items to be distributed among the other mice that had accompanied him to the monastery. Because of his extraordinary power to jump and supernatural power to move he could get access to the bowl wherever the monk tried to hide it. In fact the source of power of Hiranyaka was his hoard of wealth he had inherited. This hoard was kept in a packet on which Hiranyaka used to sleep and the power of wealth thus got instilled in him endowing him with power unnatural for any mouse. The monk did his best to hide the bowl by shifting it from place to place and to drive out the mouse by a bamboo stick. But all his efforts failed because of supernatural power from wealth of the mouse. The monk could never explain the source of supernatural power of the mouse. So, Hiranyaka and his followers went on living happily at the cost of the mendicant monk. But this happiness did not last long. One day, a friend of the monk called Brihadasphika came to the monastery and stayed there as a guest. At night in bed while the guest was discussing serious religious matters with his host he found the latter to be unmindful and hitting here and there with a long bamboo stick. He considered this to be neglect of him out of pride of the host and this made him extremely angry. He abused his host with harsh words and resolved to leave the monastery at once because of being humiliated. Butakarna then begged apology and explained to his guest the reason for his un-mindfulness. Hearing all these, Brihadasphika thought for some time and told his friend that there ought to be some source of supernatural power of the mouse. In this connection he told his host the story of mother Sandilee the essence of which is that if a person has something uncommon to his nature or capabilities there ought to be some secret and special reason behind it. He said, "My friend this mouse has some power never to be seen in a mouse. So there ought to be some specific source of his extraordinary power. We are to find out his burrow and digging it we may discover that special source of power of this mouse. Anyway, does he come alone or with his companions?" Butakarna replied, "The mouse comes with other mice as did tonight". Brihadasphika said "O.K. they may assemble here from various places but after getting food they must return direct to their burrows. Next morning by following their paw marks we would be able to find out their place of residence". At that moment Hiranyaka and the other mice in their hiding places were ready to go back to the fortress, their residence. Hearing the intelligent guest, Hiranyaka decided not to leave behind any paw mark. So he guided his mice followers by a new roundabout route through grasses where no paw mark would be left. Unfortunately this path was unsafe and they were attacked by a cat. Some mice were killed and many others injured. Hiranyaka himself could escape unhurt and did not return to the fortress immediately. Other silly mice went directly to the fortress leaving behind blood marks by the injured ones. Next morning following the blood marks the Brahmanas could easily find out the fortress of the mice. Digging randomly the burrows of the mice by a pickaxe they could ultimately find out the hoard of wealth, the source of power of Hiranyaka. Brihadasphika laughed and said to his friend that this hoard was the secret source of power of the mouse. He said with conviction, "We are now taking away this hoard and henceforth the mouse would become an ordinary one losing all his extraordinary powers. Therefore you would no longer have mouse menace."

Exactly this happened next night. Hiranyaka got into the monastery as usual. He tried to jump up to reach the alms bowl. But he fell down after jumping a little height and this caused sarcastic laughter from the two Brahmanas. Later on, deep at night, he found the monks in deep slumber and Butakarna sleeping with his hoard under his pillow. Hiranyaka, in a desperate attempt to regain his wealth, picked a whole in the pillow. But one of the monks got awake and hit him hard with the bamboo stick. So he returned to the fortress injured. He realized that with the loss of wealth he had lost also his power to collect food for himself and his followers. Soon the other mice realized that Hiranyaka no longer possessed wealth and therefore the power to provide them food. So they rejected his leadership and left him.

Penniless, powerless, friendless Hiranyaka became extremely depressed and lost all interest in mundane life. In the meantime Chitragriva, entrapped along with other doves, came to seek his help. Being freed they left and thereafter Laghupatanaka, the crow sought his friendship. Friendship of Laghupatanaka gave him some solace. Now he had come to a new place and got another friend, Mantharaka. Still he was unable to shake off his sorrow of being penniless.

Lessons: i) In the mundane world wealth is the source of power of a man. A man with wealth is respected in the society irrespective of his qualities.

ii) People are attracted to a wealthy person and accept him as leader easily.

iii) Once a person loses his wealth he loses his power and his followers and dependants leave him.

23a. Mother Sandilee and Her Spoilt Sesame Seeds

Sub-story: Brihadasphika, the guest Brahmana to Butakarna, the mendicant Brahmana

A Brahmana said to his wife known as Mother Sandilee, "Tomorrow Winter Solstice would start. I would not be at home as I would have to go to the houses of my disciples so as to collect lucrative largesse. So please take the responsibility of feeding at least one Brahmana to perform the ritual of Winter Solstice, i.e. the worship of the sun god."

The Brahmani complained that there was almost nothing in the poor household to feed a Brahmana properly. At this the Brahmana advised her to perform the ritual in accordance with their capacity, whatever little the offer could be In this connection he told his wife the story of the greedy jackal.

Next day, after the Brahmana had left, the Brahmani found some sesame seeds in the house. She thought that with these seeds she could make sesame cakes to be offered to a Brahmana. For this purpose, she soaked the seeds in worm water, hulled them and in order to get them dried sprayed them on a mattress. Unfortunately a dog pissed on the seeds. Mother Sandilee was very much upset and could not think what else she could offer to a Brahmana as there was nothing else in the house to offer to a Brahmana. Suddenly an idea came to her mind. She carried the spoilt seeds on a winnowing pot and started asking the householders in the locality if anyone was willing to exchange unhulls sesame seeds for her hulled ones. She explained that this deal was a part of a brata (religious ritual). One Brahmana housewife accepted the profitable offer and got her unhulled seeds exchanged for the hulled ones offered by Mother Sandilee. After the husband of this Brahmani had returned home he learnt about the exchange and asked from whom the hulled seeds had been taken. While he heard that it was from Mother Sandilee he told that a shrewd woman like Mother Sandilee would never make such unprofitable exchange unless there were some evil intentions. The exchange was contrary to the nature of the shrewd lady and there must be some reason behind it. So he asked his wife to throw away the hulled sesame seeds taken from Mother Sandilee.

Lessons: i) Unusual behaviour, contrary to the nature of a person, always has some hidden reason behind it. And therefore, this type of behaviour of a person should always be suspected and handled with caution.

23a-1. The Greedy Jackal

Chain Story: The Brahmana to his wife Mother Sandilee

A hunter of the Pulinda tribe went for hunting as usual. In the deep forest he suddenly came upon a wild boar at a distance. The boar was overwhelmingly large and menacing. The sight of the horrible boar panicked the hunter who thought it to be the agent of death god. Still he gathered courage and hit the boar with arrow. The injured boar too charged the hunter with its sharp task and tore his belly. Both the hunter and the boar died at the spot. Soon a jackal in quest of food arrived at the spot and was extremely elated to find such a vast amount of food at a single spot. He decided to eat every bit of these food items over a long period of time. Nothing could be left over or wasted. So he decided to start eating from the string of the hunter's bow.

With this plan in mind the greedy jackal started chewing one end of the bow-string. Soon the string snapped leading to sudden expansion of the bow. In an instant the end of the bow pierced through the mouth of the jackal and came out of his head. The greedy jackal died in a moment.

Lessons: i) Excessive greed leads to disaster.

24. The Fate of Praptabyamartha, the Son of the Merchant

Hiranyaka to Laghupatanaka and Mantharaka

In a city there lived a merchant named Sagardatta. His son was a bit foolish. One day he purchased a book from a vendor at 100 rupees. The book contained only one sloka that meant:

A person ought to get the wealth or anything else which is predestined for him. No divine power can alter this destiny. For this reason I neither ponder nor is surprised over anything I get or fail to get. What is destined to be mine can by no means be of others.

To find that his son had wasted so much money for a book with just one sloka the merchant got overwhelmingly angry and ordered the foolish son to leave his house and never to come back again. Utterly humiliated and with a painful heart the boy left the city and soon reached another city. Here he started doing odd jobs for living. He was a new comer to the place. So many persons asked him about his whereabouts and reason for leaving his own city. To all such queries he had only one brief reply "Praptabyamartha" (the wealth you are destined to have). He said nothing more and used to sleep at night in desolate temples or abandoned buildings. Soon, everyone of this place started calling him by the nickname, Praptabya. So he went on living by doing odd jobs that happened to come his way.

One day, Chandramati, the princess of the country to which that city belonged, was watching with her friends from the balcony of her room the passersby of the street close to the palace. She was young, radiant with beauty and because of full youth having a lovelorn heart desiring for someone to fulfill her desire. By coincidence, an extremely handsome prince of another country was passing by that road at that time. The glance of Chandramati fell on the prince and by the conspiracy of the god of love she fell madly in love with the prince and desired to get the prince in no time. With such a love-infected mind she told everything to her friends and asked one of her friends to hand over her letter to the prince immediately. In the letter she had written, "Hey, handsome prince, I am the princess of this country and fallen madly in love with you at first sight. I feel I cannot love anybody else and I am unable to live without you. So please accept my offer of love and meet me this night in my room so that we may get our love fulfilled." After the friend had handed over the letter to the prince he walked back and looked from the street at the princess on the balcony and he too got enchanted with her beauty. He asked the messenger how to get at the room of the princess. At this the girl said that at mid night he would find a ladder of woven leather hanging from the balcony of the palace. By this he could easily climb up to the balcony and thereafter through the door kept open would be able to enter into the room of the princess. After thinking over the pros and cons of the matter the prince thought that this adventure would be a grave sin. So he decided not to undertake the love venture. He left the place and did not keep the promised made to the messenger of the princess At night while Praptabya was roaming along the street he found the ladder hanging from the balcony of the royal palace and out of curiosity climbed up the ladder and entered the room of the princess. In semi darkness the passion ridden princess took Praptabya to be her prince and embraced and kissed him deeply and went on asking him many things. Praptabya thought this to be predestined and at last recited the sloka. Hearing this awkward sloka from the person in her embrace, the princess realized at once that she had hugged and kissed a wrong person. She felt utterly ashamed of this accidental act on her part, and immediately abused and forced Praptabya down the ladder.

Once again the poor boy started roaming along the street in quest of a place for night stay. He soon discovered a ruined temple and decided to sleep inside it. However, a police man had already selected this place for his secret meeting with a whore. As Praptabya reached the temple and told the police that he wanted to sleep there. Realising that he was a harmless vagabond, the policeman asked Praptabya to go to his own house and sleep in his drawing room instead of the temple. Praptabya could find out the house of the police as directed by the latter. With the key given by the police he opened the door of the house of the police and by mistake, instead of entering the drawing room he entered into the room of the daughter of the policeman. In the absence of her father the daughter had invited her lover to her room. She too mistook Praptabya as her lover and took him into bed in order to make love. This too appeared to the boy to be destined for him, and he at once uttered the sloka which made this girl too realize that a wrong person had entered her room. And she did not waste time in driving him out of her room. Now, once again Praptabya continued roaming along the main street in order to find some suitable nook for sleeping.

It was now almost dawn and Praptabya was amazed to find at some distance on the street a pompous marriage procession with music and light and an elephant carrying some items for marriage. Suddenly a sound of crackers from the procession made the elephant panicked. It soon killed the climber and charged through the procession. Everybody fled living only the bride at the mercy of the crazy elephant. Praptabya saw this and he felt a deep urge to save the helpless bride from the crazy elephant. With extraordinary boldness he dashed in between the bride and the elephant, held the shivering bride in embrace with his right hand and addressed the elephant in an admonishing tone, "You foolish elephant, don't do any harm to this helpless bride and leave this place at once". As though by some magic, the elephant became calm and left the place. Soon, as the danger was over, every one of the marriage party returned to the spot. The groom got angry to find his bride in the arms of another man. He started admonishing the father of the girl by saying that the latter had cheated him by offering the girl to another person. The perplexed father of the bride said that he did not know anything of this as he too had fled while the elephant had been on rampage. The girl announced boldly that she could marry only her brave savior and not any coward like the groom arranged by her father. Now Praptabya started uttering the sloka. It was already morning. A large number of persons gathered around the place. The daughter of the policeman and the princess along with the king also came to the spot. At the request of the king a scholar interpreted the meaning of the sloka to the king. Querying Praptabya, the king got the detail of his story. The king then gave immunity to the daughter of the policeman and the bride from any social stigma, promised them financial rewards and offered the princess in marriage to Praptabya along with a grant of 1000 villages.

Lessons: i) What a man would get in life is pre-destined and nothing can change this. One in his life would get neither more nor less than what is fixed by destiny for him.

25. Samilak, the Weaver and the God of Fate

Mantharaka to Hiranya and Laghupatanaka

In a certain city there lived a weaver named Samilak. He was an expert weaver capable of weaving various categories of high quality fabrics. But in spite of his skill his income was barely enough to make provision of a very simple house for living, simple clothes and essential food for himself and his wife. But many weavers of the locality with low level of skill could earn much more than him enabling them to provide for luxuries. Samilak, therefore, thought that remaining in that place he would never be able to earn anything more. Only a change of place could enable him to earn more. He had seen many persons endowed with fortune after moving on to other places. So he decided to try his luck at some new place. His wife, however, protested against his decision. She tried her best to convince Samilak that there is nothing wrong in the place of their residence, but it was his destiny that was not permitting him to earn more. So a change of place was not likely to change his fate. But Samilak did not pay heed to what his wife had said and soon left the place and moved to a new city called Vardhamana. With much effort of three years he could save 300 gold coins. Thereafter he left for home with his saved wealth kept in a bag. On the way, night fell while he was inside a forest. For safety, Samilak climbed up a tree, lay down on a wide reclined branch and fell asleep. Soon he had a dream. In his dream he heard two gods conversing at the bottom of the tree. The god Deed blamed the god Doer by saying, "Why have you let this man earn 300 gold coins whereas he, by fate, is entitled to nothing more than bare necessities like food, shelter and clothing for himself and his family?" Doer replied, "My duty is to reward a person according to his labour. I have done exactly my duty. Now the rest lies at your hand." Samilak's sleep broke and examining his bag of coins he found it empty.

He got much depressed to find his purse empty and thought that it would be meaningless to return home empty handed. He wanted to try his luck again. So he returned to Vardhamana and now with very hard labour saved 500 gold coins in one year only. This time, while returning home, he followed a different path to avoid the forest. But surprisingly as soon as night fell he found himself under the same tree. And now from a little distance he saw the same two figures at the bottom of the tree. He now, in wakeful condition, heard their conversation. The god Deed blamed the god Doer by saying, "Why have you let this man earn 500 gold coins whereas he, by fate, is not entitled to anything more than bare necessities like food, shelter and clothing for himself and his family?" Doer replied as before, "My duty is to reward a person according to his labour. I have done exactly my duty. Now the rest lies at your hand." The gods vanished and Samilak found his bag of gold coins empty again. Now he was extremely depressed. How could he return home empty handed and show his face to his wife? With this thought Samilak decided to commit suicide by hanging himself from a branch of the tree. To this end he prepared a noose with a strong creeper as the hanging rope. At the moment he was going to hang himself, the god Deed prevented him from doing so. He told Samilak that he had been pleased at the determination of Samilak and requested him to ask for a boon. Samilak said, "If you want to give me a boon give me please immense wealth." The god said, "What use of wealth if you cannot enjoy it yourself because of your destiny?" Samilak replied that possession of wealth alone has attraction and emanates power whether one may enjoy it or not. To explain his view he told the god the story of the Bull and the Vixen.

Thereafter the god suggested Samilak to meet first two persons of different characters, Guptadhana and Upabhuktadhana, having wealth in two different ways. Thereafter decide which type of wealth ownership he prefered.as a boon. The god disappeared and on the basis of directions given by the god, Samilak first found out the city where Guptadhana lived. Then Samilak went to the house of Guptadhana. It was very difficult to make entry into the house as Guptadhana tried to prevent his entry. But he could not prevent the adamant Samilak from entering the house. Then Samilak was served very low quality food for dinner in a broken plate and provided only a straw bed at the veranda for sleeping at night. At mid night his sleep broke and he heard the conversation of the two gods again. Deed complained to Doer for permitting this man to spend more than he should by destiny by providing food to the weaver. Doer replied that he had done only his duty and the rest is at the hand of Deed. Next day Guptadhana had a severe diarrhea, no food was to be prepared and thereby the amount he had spent for Samilak was recovered. Leaving the house of Guptadhana, Samilak found out the house of Upabhuktadhana. He was now cordially welcome by the host, offered delicious food and cozy bed for sleeping at night. This night too, the two gods appeared. Deed blamed Doer, "Why have you permitted this person to spend so much while he has already spent all his resources?" Doer replied as before, "I have simply discharged my duty. The rest is with you." Next morning penniless Upabhuktadhana got a gift of a large amount of money from the king. This enabled him to spend again for the benefit of other persons. Samilak left this house and took his decision about the choice of the boon. That night the god appeared before Samilak and asked him about his choice. At this Samilak expressed his desire to be like Upabhuktadhana, having immense wealth to be spent for others. The god gave him the wealth and left.

Lessons: I) Fate is the final deciding factor as regards what a person would earn.

25a. Tikhnashringa, the Bull and the Greedy Vixen

Sub-story: Samilak, the weaver to the god of Fate

In a town closed to a forest there was a group of bulls. Among them a bull called Tikhnashringa (sharp horn) was extremely strong and had very large hanging testicles. Because of his strength he despised the other bulls and therefore left the herd and started roaming alone along the lush grassland close to the forest.

One day while the bull was grazing, a fox and a vixen happened to see him close to the place of their hunting rats and other small animals. The vixen glanced at the hanging testicles of the bull and from their condition she expected that these two lumps of flesh would soon drop down. "Oh, what a delicious food they would be! This would relieve me from the boredom of eating rats and tasteless insects", she thought. She told this to her husband and requested him to follow the bull so that they could get access to the balls of delicious meat as soon as the fleshy balls drop down. The fox was reluctant to leave the place of their hunting as it was uncertain if the balls would at all fall down. But because of continuous entreaty of his wife he, along with the vixen, started following the bull from place to place. They wasted several years in hope but the balls remained where they had been. The jackal realized that the balls were firm and would never drop down and they had simply wasted time over something uncertain.

Lessons: ii) Wealth as such has attraction to most of the persons. Whether it is procurable or not people still hang around wealth.

26. The Mice and the Entrapped Elephants

Chitranga to Mantharaka, Hiranyaka and Laghupatanaka

In an abandoned town close to a forest there was a vast colony of mice with thousands of mice living in burrows. There was a beautiful lake close by. Many small animals from the forest used to visit the lake for drinking fresh and cool water. Once a herd of elephants, in quest of drinking water, discovered the lake and in order to meet thirst rushed towards the lake trampling a part of the colony of the mice. Many mice were killed and many others injured in this sudden onslaught of the thirsty elephants. The elephants returned to the forest and decided to stay in the proximity of drinking water. The mice realised that these elephants were likely to follow the same path every day and soon all the mice would be trampled by them. In order to find a way out of this impending disaster, the mice held a meeting and their leaders decided to request the elephant king to follow a different route to the lake so that the mice colony was not destroyed. They approached the king elephant and was capable of convincing him to follow with his group a different path avoiding the mouse colony. The mice promised to the elephants that they should not hesitate to seek help of the mice if needed in future. The king of the elephants thanked them and said laughing that such small animals are not likely to be of any help to large animals like them.

But soon something happened that made the elephants seek help of the mice. Sometimes later hunters of the king captured by decoying device most of the bull elephants along with their king. They tied the elephants with large trees with very strong ropes and left to the tent for lunch. The king of the elephants could recognise the place and remembered that the mouse colony was close by. So he requested a cow elephant that had not been captivated to contact the mice and seek their help. The cow elephant soon ran to the mice colony and informed the mice about the captivity of the elephants. Thousands of mice soon approached the spot and in a trice set the elephants free by cutting off the ropes to bits.

Lessons: i) Small and apparently insignificant persons could be of help to a powerful person under certain circumstances. So, one should not hesitate to strike up friendship with any person with a good heart but apparently less powerful or insignificant as compared to him.

27. Captivity of Chitranga and Hazard of Mantharaka

One day Chitranga failed to appear in the group meeting in time. After waiting some time the other friends apprehended that he must have got into some trouble. Laghupatanaka flew high and moved around to find out Chitranga and soon he discovered Chitranga entrapped at a place close by in a hunter's noose. The crow dropped down to Chitranga and assured him that soon he would bring over there on his back Hiranyaka so as to get the trap cut off by him. Then the crow returned to the group and carried Hiranyaka on his back to the spot where the deer was entrapped. Before leaving, both of them had requested Mantharaka not to accompany them because in case of trouble a slow moving animal like him would be unable to escape. While the crow and the mouse arrived at the spot Hiranyaka got ready to gnaw at the cords of the trap. In the meantime Chitranga related to them the story of his childhood captivity.

While they were talking, they found the hunter approaching the trap with a club in his hand. Unfortunately at that very moment Mantharaka also arrived at the spot as he could not bear the worry for Chitranga. Hiranyaka cut off the cords of the trap. Chitranga ran away fast, the crow flew up on a tree branch and the mouse hid in a reed bed. Unfortunately, the hunter could catch Mantharaka, who failed to escape, tied him with grass ropes and considered him to be a compensation for the lost deer. Carrying the tied tortoise on his shoulder the hunter proceeded for his residence. However, the other friends hatched up a plan to rescue Mantharaka. They followed the hunter up to a water body. As planned beforehand, the deer lay like a dead one with the crow sitting on his body feigning to pick out his eyes. The hunter got elated to find a dead deer. He dropped Mantharaka on the ground and ran towards Chitranga. In an instant Hiranyaka cut off the rope binding Mantharaka who immediately escaped into water, Chitranga ran away fast before the hunter could reach him, Hiranyaka hid in a crevice and Laghupatanaka flied high up. The incident was so unprecedented that the hunter thought it to be a bad omen and ran away for his residence as fast as he could.

Lessons: i) Inadvertence may lead to trouble. Fate also may be responsible for predicaments. But with the help of intelligent friends with appropriate planning problems could be overcome.

Chapter-4: Tantra III-War of Attrition between the Crows and the Owls

Primary Story: Shrewd Maneuvers of the Old Crow and Destruction of the Owls

Close to the south Indian city of Prithibipratisthana, there was a gigantic banyan tree. This was the habitation of a large number of crows. The name of their king was Meghavarna. At some distance from this tree lived the great and powerful owl king named Arimardana with a large number of owls in a cave fortress of a mountain. Crows are the natural enemies of the owls. So every evening when the day-blind owls were capable of seeing, they used to move up to the banyan tree and killed many crows. The crow king Meghavarna got very much worried about this. He had no idea about the location of the fortress of the owls who were physically more powerful than the crows. In order to save his subjects from extinction Meghavarna thought of devising some plan to save the crows from the relentless attacks of the powerful owls.

To this end he summoned his five ministers to a conference in order to get their advices in this regard. The five ministers were – Ujjivi, Sanjivi, Anujivi, Projivi and Chiranjivi. The retired minister and a great statesman, the old Sthirajivi, was also invited as an observer. In the conference, Meghavarna started seeking the opinions of his ministers one by one.

At first he sought the opinion of Ujjivi who opined that hostilities against the powerful enemies should be avoided. So the best means would be conciliation. The minister Sanjivi opposed the opinion of Ujjivi. He said that cruel owls would never accept the offer of peace. So the best means would be to wage total war against them. While asked, Anujivi opined that neither peace nor war was desirable under the circumstances. The owls would not accept the offer of peace. On the other hand, war with such a powerful enemy would lead to complete annihilation of the crows. So the best means would be to abandon this tree and withdraw to a new place which is safe from the attacks of the owls. The minister Projivi opined that neither offer of peace nor direct war nor retreat is desirable. The best way would be to stand united and resist the attacks of the owls jointly in a defensive manner. The minister Chiranjivi objected to the opinions of the earlier four ministers and said that an alliance with some other birds in order to fight jointly against the mighty owls would be the best conceivable solution to the problem. To this end the crows should find out some suitable allies.

Now Meghavarna turned to the old crow Sthirajivi who had served as a minister of his father and was a great statesman and diplomat. Sthirajivi said calmly that all the five ministers had expressed their views according to political expedience, but under the present circumstances none of them was likely be effective. The only way out in the situation appeared to be pursuance of the deceitful diplomacy of double standard. He promised to take responsibility of accomplishing the scheme at his own risk.

He went on, "Oh my king, now the most important task is to find out the fortress of the owls and through espionage activity ascertain the strength and weakness of the enemy. I would also have knowledge of the high officials of both the sides through spies." At the query of Meghavarna, Sthirajivi gave details of 18 important officials in enemy's ranks and 15 in their own ranks.

Thereafter Meghavarna expressed curiosity about the reason for natural enmity between the crows and the owls. Then Sthirajivi gave a detail account of the origin of natural enmity between the crows and the owls: the story of The Origin of Crow-Owl Enmity. . Thereafter he took Meghavarna aside and related to him the detail of his deceitful scheme.

The Scheme of Thirajivi: It would start with a got up quarrel and fight between Meghavarna and Sthirajivi. Meghavarna would adopt a mock hostile attitude towards Sthirajivi blaming him as a spy of the owls. Soon the quarrel would turn violent and Meghavarna would attack Sthirajivi, injure him a little and through him down to the bottom of the tree. To exaggerate his injury, blood collected from somewhere would be smeared on his entire body. All these should be done in a manner that the spies of the owls were convinced that the king of the crow had really attacked and severely injured an old minister and there was a dispute among the crows. Thus preparing the trap for deceiving the owls, Meghavarna with all the crows should immediately fly far off to the Antelope Hill. This should be done just before evening. So being informed of the incident through spies the owl king Arimardana must approach the banyan tree to examine what exactly had happened to his enemies. In order to get idea about the new shelter of the crows Arimardana would for sure pay attention to the injured and aggrieved Sthirajivi and being fooled by the deceitful activity of the latter would give him shelter. Then it would be easy for Sthirajivi to device schemes to destroy the owls. At first, considering the high risk for the life of Sthirajivi, Meghavarna expressed reluctance to accept the plan. But ultimately Sthirajivi was able to convince his king to accept the plot.

Exactly according to the plan, right before evening, Meghavarna picked up a mock quarrel with Sthirajivi blaming in stentorian voice that the latter was a traitor and spy of the owls. Soon his voice became louder and louder and ultimately he attacked and injured the old crow and threw him down to the bottom of the banyan tree. As preplanned some crows sprayed blood on the entire body of Sthirajivi. After this the crows along with their king did not waste time to fly away to the Antelope Hill. Soon the owl-spies informed the queen, the chief of the owl espionage network, about the incident. The queen in no time informed the matter to Arimardana. Arimardana got highly elated to learn about the dispute and fight among the crows. It was already dark and everything visible to the day-blind owls. Arimardana with five of his ministers soon arrived at the spot. The owls found that all the crows have left the place except the severely injured old crow who, from the bottom of the tree, was crying and lamenting madly. When the owls attempted to kill the injured crow, Arimardana dissuaded them. He thought that this crow being tortured by his king may help him find out the whereabouts of the crows and also provide him all the secrets of the crows. While Arimardana got closer to the injured crow the latter cried aloud and requested Arimardana to kill him. He said that death is better than such physical pain and humiliation by the king of the crows whom he had served loyally since the time of the father of this king. Asked why the king did so to him, Sthirajivi said that he had simply requested him not to get into war with the stronger owls but to appeal to the owls for peace. Arimardana was easily fooled by the trick of the old crow and decided to save this crow and find out information about the crows from this aggrieved old crow. He asked his five ministers about what to do with this injured crow. The minister Raktaksha opined that the enemy should be exterminated immediately. He said that love once broken could never be restored. Enmity between the owls and the crows would never come to an end. So owls ought not to trust a crow. To corroborate his view he told the story of the Brahmana and the Gold Paying Snake.

Next Arimardana sought the opinion of the minister Kruraksha who opined that a person even if belonging to the enemy camp should be given shelter when he is in distress. So the injured crow should be given shelter. In this connection he told the story of the Hunter and the Doves.

The minister Diptaksha opined that an advantage even if from an enemy should not be ignored. So the injured crow should be given shelter in order to learn about the whereabouts of the other crows. In this context he told the story of the Old Man, Young Wife and the Thief.

The minister Vakranasa opined that the injured crow should be given shelter in order to take advantage of the quarrelling enemies.

To corroborate his conviction he told the story of the Brahmana, the Robber and the Demon. The minister Prakarkarna opined that the old crow should not be killed. He expected that soon friendship would develop between Arimardana and the old crow and the crow, in course of friendly talks, would disclose to Arimardana the secrets of the crows. He then told the story of the Serpent in the Belly of the Prince.

Arimardana decided to accept the majority view rejecting the views of Raktaksha who alone among them had idea of realpolitik and diplomacy and the tricks of Sthirajivi failed to fool him. So Arimardana decided not to kill the old crow but to give him shelter in their fortress. Raktaksha, realising the oncoming danger to the owls, tried his best to convince again his king and the other ministers of the danger of giving shelter to the enemy. To convince them he told the story of the Chariot Maker Cuckolded by His Wife. But the foolish owls disregarded once again the warnings of Raktaksha.

Arimardana ordered the owls to carry the injured crow safely to the fortress. On the way Sthirajivi continued with his deceitful drama. He requested Arimardana to throw him into fire and get him killed instead of giving him safe shelter. Raktaksha felt how shrewd the old crow was. He asked the crow mockingly why he wanted to immolate himself. Sthirajivi replied that he desired to take rebirth as an owl and take revenge against the crows who had done such injustice to him. Raktaksha retorted by praising the diplomatic quality of the crow and said that even if he would take rebirth as an owl, he would remain an enemy of the owls and friend of the crows. In this connection he told the story of the Mouse-Maiden and the Sage Yajnavalka. Arimardana and other ministers disregarded the aggrieved Raktaksha who realized that because of their folly the owls are going to invite a very serious disaster to the entire owl community.

Arriving at the cave fortress Arimardana ordered his attendants to prepare a chamber inside the fort for cozy living of the injured crow. Sthirajivi realised that living inside the fort among the owls would deprive him of proceeding with his secret activities to destroy the owls. So he protested by saying, "Oh owl king, I am highly gratified at your magnanimity. But I am still an outsider and it is not justified to permit an outsider to stay right inside your fortress. So please arrange for my stay outside the gate of the cave. From this place I would provide my service to your honour every day"

This proposal appeared proper for Arimardana. By his order the owl attendants arranged for stay of the old crow outside the mouth of the cave fortress. With sumptuous food and adequate rest Sthirajivi soon became fully cured of the injuries and he became stout and strong. Now he had plenty of time to plan the scheme to destroy the owls.

Observing the activities of the old crow Raktaksha could anticipate the impending disaster for the owl race. He did his last effort to bring to the notice of his king and other owls the impending disaster. He presented himself in the full court of the king and told the story of the Bird that Dropped Golden Turd and attempted to convince the king and other owls that they all had been fooled by the old crow. But none attached any importance to what the dissenting minister had deliberated in the court. Raktaksha then gathered together his kins and faithful followers, made them convinced of the impending danger to the owls community in that place and he along with all his kins and followers flew to another mountain cave.

Departure of Raktaksha gave much relief to Sthirajivi as he knew that Raktaksha was the lone owl minister who could suspect the sinister plots of him. Now under the pretext of building his home outside the cave Sthirajivi soon gathered a great pile of dry leaves and dry tree branches. During day time while the owls were sleeping, he flew fast to the Antelope Hill and informed Meghavarna about his preparations and requested that all the crows should in no time carry burning twigs and set fire to the pile at the mouth of the owl cave. All the crows followed his directions and soon a great fire developed at the mouth of the cave and all the day-blind owls were roasted alive. In this manner by sheer statecraft and deceitful diplomacy of the old crow the physically weaker crows could destroy their powerful owl enemies. Thereafter the crows returned to the banyan tree, their old home, now free from any owl menace. While relating to Meghavarna and other crows his experience in the company of the enemies and how he waited for the appropriate moment of action, Sthirajivi told them the story of the Snake that Carried the Frogs on His Back.' Thereafter he gave a philosophical discourse on the role of Time in creating and dissolving events of history.

Lessons:

i) Diplomacy and intelligence are more powerful than physical strength.

ii) One should never trust and give shelter to an agent of his natural enemy.

Secondary Stories
28. The Origin of Crow-Owl Enmity

Sthirajivi, the wise old crow to Meghavarna, the king of the crows

Once, the assembly of the birds had decided to coronate a local king who would look after the well-being of the birds on earth. Their king Lord Gadura resides in far off Vaikuntha to serve his master Lord Vishnu. So he is incapable of meeting the immediate needs of the birds. The assembly of the birds unanimously selected the owl, a very strong bird, as their local king. Accordingly they arranged for a ceremony and completed all the rituals necessary for coronation of the owl leader as their king. The chosen owl rode to the lion-throne placed on a raised dais and was ready for being coronated by the bird-priest as the local king of the birds. Right at that moment a crow, who could not join the assembly on time, entered the scene. Asking the birds about the reason for the gorgeous ceremony he learnt about the coronation of the owl as their local king.

Hearing all these, the crow spontaneously laughed aloud and started putting strong arguments against the owl as a person for such important position. In fact, the crow did this without deep thinking and without having any prior enmity with the owls. He did this on the spur of the moment. As regards his objections, the crow mentioned various drawbacks of the owl some of which were: i) The Owl is an extremely ugly bird.

ii) He is day-blind.

iii) He is very cruel and fierce in nature. So he is likely to do more harm than benefits to the birds.

The crow also opined that the birds already had a great king like Lord Gadura. So a second king was not at all desirable. When the other birds argued that Lord Gadura resides at a distant place and cannot come to the immediate help of the birds in need, the crow argued that the name of a great king like Lord Gadura is enough for the birds to be rescued from any jeopardy. To corroborate his view he told the story of the Hare, the Elephant King and the Moon God.

Thereafter, to explain the mischievous nature of the owl the crow told the story of the Hypocrite Cat

Being convinced by the arguments of the crow all the birds, who had assembled for the coronation ceremony, abandoned the ceremony and left the place leaving the depressed owl alone. The abandoned owl learnt that the reason for his humiliation was the wickedness of the crow. Since then owls became the natural enemies of the crows.

The crow, who had spoilt the coronation ceremony, soon came to senses and realized that because of his foolish activity for no justifiable reason at all, he had created a permanent natural enemy of the race of crows.

Lessons: i) Inadvertent activity and silly deeds at the spur of the moment may lead to permanent harm like creating permanent natural enemies.

28a. The Hare, the Elephant King and the Moon God

Sub Story-1: The Crow to the Assembly of Birds in the coronation ceremony of the owl

There lived in a forest an elephant king named Chaturdanta. There were a large number of elephants under his command. Suddenly prolonged drought led to severe water scarcity in that part of the forest. The king elephant sent his agents to find out some source of adequate drinking water. After long searches the elephants came upon a beautiful fresh water lake known as Moon Lake. The surroundings were beautiful and lush green foliage indicated that the place was nourished with regular rain. They returned and informed this to their king. Then Chaturdanta with all his retinues moved towards that attractive place. After shifting to the forest surrounding the lake, the elephants felt thirsty. They proceeded to water along the sloppy sides of the lake. But in these slopes there were the burrows of many hares. The rushing elephants damaged the burrows of the hares, crushing and killing many hares. Soon the surviving hares held a meeting. They apprehended that these elephants were likely to rush to the lake-water again and again exterminating all the surviving hares. Some of the hares advised their king that it would be safe for them to leave the place and settle somewhere else. The king, however, was unwilling to abandon their ancestral home. So he summoned Lambakarna, a very shrewd diplomat and expert in deceitful activities against enemies. Listening carefully to the problem, Lambakarna assured his king and other hares that he would by some cunning device make the elephants leave this place for ever. To this end he would meet the king of the elephants and get him frightened by a deceitful device.

Lambakarna soon arrived at the part of the forest where the elephants were expected to have settled. After some searching he could find out the king of the elephants. For his safety he climbed upon a mound close to the elephant camp but not accessible to the elephants. From the safe place he addressed the elephant king loudly, "Hey elephant king, you have committed an unpardonable sin by killing the hares and destroying their homes while rushing towards the water of the lake." The elephant king asked who he was. Lambakarna said that he was the messenger of the Moon god who had become vehemently angry with the elephants for killing his dearest animals, the hares. The god would soon punish all the mischievous elephants. The elephant king knew that hares are favourites of the Moon god as there is a hare on the body of the god. So he got frightened and asked how he could be forgiven by the god. Lambakarna replied that Chaturdanta would have to beg apology to the god and then promise never to come again to the lake. The elephant now wanted to see the god so that he could beg apology. It was already evening and fortunately a full moon night. There was a reflection of the moon inside the clean water of the lake. So the cunning hare led the elephant king to the lake and showed him the image of the moon in the water of the lake. The elephant king was thus fooled and begged apology to the moon image in the lake water and thereafter he with his retinues left the place never to come back again.

Lessons: i) A shrewd person can easily fool an enemy much powerful than him.

ii) Simply the mention of God makes many persons frightened and prevents them from undertaking mischievous activities.

28b. The Hypocrite Cat and His Victims

Sub Story-2: The Crow to the Assembly of Birds in the coronation ceremony of the owl

In a large crevice close to the trunk of a tree lived a partridge. Once he left his home and flew into a new place where profuse grains of various categories were freely available. Attraction of these grains kept the bird stuck at the new place for several years. On the other hand, a few months after the partridge had left his home, a hare came to that place. Finding and empty crevice of the tree he decided to make it his home. For several years there was no problem. But a few years later the partridge remembered his home and decided to return to his old home. But coming back to the old place he found his house occupied by a hare. He requested the hare to vacate the house but the hare declined claiming that there was no proof that it was the house of the bird.

Moreover he mentioned a rule that long occupancy of a house gives the right of ownership to the occupant. Soon quarrel ensured between the partridge and the hare. The other birds that gathered around them could not give any verdict as they did not have deep knowledge of legal provisions in such a situation. At last both the disputing parties agreed to look for a wise person who could give proper verdict on the dispute. Both of them travelled a long way and at last arrived at a river bank. They found at some distance a cat meditating with closed eyes under a banyan tree. He looked very wise. So they agreed to approach this wise person for solution of their problem. Both of them knew that a cat is a ferocious and hunter animal. So they stood at safe distance and addressed the cat. The cat got elated to find two lucrative preys. When the cat asked why they had beckoned him, the hare and the partridge told the cat that they had a dispute and they expected that the wise cat would be able to resolve it. At the same time they did not fail to express their apprehensions that the cat may as well do them harm as natural for cats. But the cat was very shrewd. After attentively listening to their apprehensions about the predatory nature of the cats, the cat said that he was completely different from ordinary cats as he had already lost interest in all mundane matters. By deceitful discourses he could fool both the hare and the partridge and was able to convince them that he was in penance, had turned into a vegetarian and vowed to god that henceforth he would never do any harm to any person. The hare and the partridge now mentioned the reason for their dispute. The cat said that because of age his hearing power was very poor. He could not fully hear what they were saying. So he requested them to relate their problem coming closer to him. The fooled partridge and hare took the cat into full trust and got closer to him with a view to giving the cat detail of the reason for their dispute. But as soon as they got near him the cat did not lose time to kill both of them simultaneously.

Lessons: i) A ferocious and deceitful animal or person like a cat should never be trusted.

ii) A third party with criminal intentions can easily take advantage of the dispute of two persons.

29. The Brahmana, His Goat and Three Rouges

The old crow Sthirajivi to king Meghavarna and other crows

A Brahmana named Mitra Sharma was presented a plump he-goat by one of his disciples for performance of sacrifice to a deity. The Brahmana started returning home with the goat on his shoulder along the path through a forest. Soon the plump animal on the shoulder of the Brahmana came to the notice of three notorious persons. They became greedy for the meat of the plump animal. They then conspired and hatched out a plan to fool the Brahmana and make him abandon the animal. They changed their dresses so that they appeared as different classes of persons and stood at some distance from one another by the side of the path.

As soon as the Brahmana got close to the first rogue he came out of the bush by the side of the road and exclaimed, "What a surprise!. A holy Brahmana like you are carrying a filthy animal like a dog on your shoulder?" Mitra Sharma considered this to be a nasty joke by some urchin. So he reprimanded the rogue and continued his journey. After some time the Brahmana got closer to the second rogue who came forward and expressed surprise in his eyes and said, "Oh Sir, it is unbelievable. Being a respectful Brahmana you are carrying a dead calf on your shoulder!" This time too, the Brahmana ignored the rogue and proceeded towards home. But soon he came upon the third rogue waiting for him on the way. Like the other two this rogue came forward and said, "Hey Holy Brahmana, are you crazy? I am horrified that a pious Brahmana is carrying on his shoulders a despicable animal like an ass."

Now the Brahmana started reflecting. Three different types of persons had said ominous things about the animal on his shoulder. So the animal could be a demon or some mischievous element. So he dropped the he-goat on the ground and rushed for home as fast as he could. Thereafter the three rogues had a good feast with the plump he-goat.

Lessons: i) Repeated lies may make falsehood appear true. So a person could be deceived by repeated lies from different persons with prior conspiracy.

30. The Ants Who Killed the Snake

The old crow Sthirajivi to king Meghavarna and other crows

A large and very strong snake lived in a burrow close to an anthill. One day while getting out of his burrow his body got injured by some sharp stones close to the mouth of the burrow. Blood started oozing out of the small wounds. The smell of blood attracted the ants from the anthill. They started climbing incessantly on the body of the injured snake and picking up blood and flesh from the wounds. In pain the snake started twisting his body in order to shake off the biting ants. He also started hitting the ants with his tail. Many ants were crushed but still remained many others. They were so innumerable and continuously coming out of their den to invade the body of the snake that ultimately the snake got completely covered with the ants and fell dead. Thereafter his body was devoured by the countless ants.

Lessons: i) A strong person may be overpowered and destroyed by weak persons who are united and innumerable.

31. The Brahmana and the Gold Paying Snake

Raktaksha, the owl minister to the owl king Arimardana

In a small town a Brahmana had a cultivable field where no crops could be grown notwithstanding the sincere efforts of the Brahmana. One day he discovered at the end of the field a mound and saw a snake residing in the mound. The Brahmana thought that it was the snake god and his field was uncultivable for not offering proper worship to this snake god. So he brought some milk in a bowl, prayed to the snake and offered it the milk. The snake at once drank the milk and dropped a gold coin in the empty bowl. Since then this went on happening every day and soon the Brahmana was free from poverty. He was not greedy and remained satisfied with one coin a day. After some time the Brahmana had to travel to a distant town to perform a ritual in the house of a disciple. So he would have to be absent from home for a few days. He, therefore, entrusted the responsibility of offering milk to the snake with his son. But his son was extremely greedy. He thought that the mound must be full of gold coins. So if he killed the snake and demolished the mound he would be able to procure all the gold coins immediately. With this mischievous design in mind he carried a cudgel hidden inside his garment when going to offer milk to the snake. As soon as the snake started drinking milk the greedy son of the Brahmana tried to hit the snake hard with the cudgel. Fortunately the snake could escape the full blow and had minor injuries only. It then attacked the son of the Brahmana and poured all his venom into the body of the boy who died instantly. The relatives of the Brahmana cremated the son. The Brahmana learnt all this after he had returned home. He put all the blame for the sad incident on his greedy son. He opined that lack of compassion for others should always be punished. To corroborate his view he told the neighbours the story of the Jealous Golden Geese of the Lotus Lake.

Next day the Brahmana approached the mound with milk bowl and begged apology to the snake for the mischief of his son. The snake declined to take the milk and said that love and trust once broken can by no means be restored.

Lessons: i) Love and Friendship once broken can by no means be restored.

31a. The Jealous Golden Geese of the Lotus Lake
Sub-story by the Brahmana to his relatives

In the kingdom of the king Chitraratha, there was a beautiful lake called Lotus Lake because the entire lake was adorned with lotus flowers of variegated colours. Soldiers of the king always guarded the lake as there lived a large number of golden geese each of whom used to pay as tribute to the king a golden tail feather every six months. The geese went on living happily.

One day a great bird, all golden, flew to the lake and requested the geese to give him shelter. He told that his nest was being invaded by a fierce fowler and he could escape by the grace of god. But the geese did not feel any pity for the helpless bird and instead of giving him shelter in the lake abused him with rude languages. The bird went on appealing to them for help but of no avail. At last the humiliated bird flew to the court of the king, explained to the king why he had been seeking shelter in the Lotus Lake and the crude and unkind way the geese had treated him. The king gave patient hearing to the complaint of the big bird and got extremely angry with the geese for their shellfish nature and unkind behaviour with the big bird seeking shelter with them. The angry king ordered his soldiers to kill all these mean hearted geese and bring their dead bodies to the court of the king.

From a distance the geese saw the soldiers approaching the lake with cudgel in hand. An old goose could grasp the predicament and according to his advice all the geese fled away in quest of a dwelling place in some new kingdom. Thus, because of their shellfish character and lack of compassion for others, the geese had to lose their old residing place.

Lessons: i) Selfishness and jealousy are baser attributes of character and should always be avoided.

32. The Fowler and the Sacrifice of the Dove

Kruraksha, a minister of the owls to his king Arimardana

A turtle-dove couple lived on a tree in a deep forest. Both of them were of noble and kind heart. Once a fierce fowler, while coursing through this forest with a view to catching birds, could entrap the dove wife and shut her in his bird-cage. But because of extremely chilly weather the fowler was shivering in cold. He was also suffering from hunger as he had taken food before leaving home long ago. Finding her enemy and captor suffering from cold and hunger the heart of the noble she-dove was filled with compassion. On the tree her husband was lamenting for the captivity of his wife. The wife heard this and shouted from inside the cage, "Please forget about my captivity. After all this fowler is a guest of ours as he has taken shelter under the tree we reside on. He is suffering from cold and hunger. So, first arrange for some fire and food for this poor fellow." This moved the heart of the noble dove. Forgetting about his wife's captivity by the fowler he too felt compassion for the suffering man. He soon flew off and came back with a burning timber lighted from the forest fire at some distance. Then he collected dry leaves and dried branches and prepared a fire that gave the fowler relief from cold. Still the hunter was hungry. So he told the fowler, "Please meet your hunger by eating my roasted body." Saying this, the dove dived into the blazing fire.

Conscience stricken, the fowler released the female dove from the cave and began to apologize for the injustice perpetrated on the dove family by him. The female dove, finding her husband burnt alive herself jumped into the fire. Soon a chariot from heaven arrived to carry the noble souls to heaven.

On the other hand the fowler felt conscience stricken. He vowed to give up his cruel profession, never to do any harm to anybody and emulate the noble doves.

Lessons: i) A noble soul possesses kindness and compassion even for his enemy.

33. Old Man, Young Wife and the Thief

Diptaksha, a minister of the owls to his king Arimardana

An old merchant was obsessed with Kama Ripu (the passion of lust) even at the age when he was physically incapable of making love with any woman. His perverted mind was looking for a wife and bribing heavily he made a poor man agree to offer his beautiful young daughter in marriage to him. The girl being forced to marry the old perverted and sexually incapable merchant became extremely unhappy and started hating the old husband from the depth of her heart. She always kept a physical distance from the old man and never permitted him to touch her. The old man always felt deep urge to embrace the soft and beautiful body of his young wife. But he never got any opportunity to fulfill his desire.

One night while the couple was sleeping in their bed room, the girl as usual at a safe distance from the old man, a thief suddenly entered into the room through the open window. The noise made by the thief's entry made both the girl and the old man awake. The girl got panicked at the sight of the thief and moving towards her husband spontaneously clasped hard the body of her husband. This thrilled the old man who had been deprived of the touch of his wife. He told the thief who was at the point of escaping through the window, "Don't be worried. You are welcome in my house. I thank you for creating the opportunity for me to be graced by the hug of my wife who would never embrace me in normal situations. I permit you to steal whatever you like from my house." The situation appeared very funny to the thief. He did not steal anything and left the house laughing.

Lessons: i) Advantage obtained even from an unwanted person should always be welcome

34. The Brahmana, the Cow-thief, and the Demon

Vakranasa, a minister of the owls to his king Arimardana

A poor widower Brahmana called Shivabhakta had two very high pedigree cows gifted by his disciples. He had no children. So he lived alone in a hut. The cows gave a good amount of milk and so they were the source of livelihood of the Brahmana. A thief discovered the lucrative cows and learnt that they were tied on a pole at night in an open shade in the courtyard of the Brahmanas. So the thief thought it would be very easy to steal the cows when the Brahmana is asleep at midnight. With this intention in mind he went out for the house of the Brahmana. Close to the house of the Brahmana the thief came upon a horrible looking demon who too was pacing in the direction of the same house. The thief got horrified to watch the demon and was about to flee when the demon assured the thief that he would do no harm to him. The demon then asked the thief about his intention of proceeding towards the house of the Brahmana. The thief replied that he was a thief and willing to steal the cows of the Brahmana. The demon said that his destination too was the house of the Brahmana but for a different purpose. He then said that he was a Brahma Rakshasa (a demon created from the soul of a Brahmana after his death). He used to eat only a Brahmana once in three days. That was the third day after his last eating and so he was going to meet his hunger by devouring this Brahmana.

Then both of them entered the house of the Brahmana. The cows were as usual tied with a pole in the courtyard and Shivabhakta was in deep slumber on a bedstead in the open verandah of the cottage. The thief said that he would steal the cows first because attempt of the demon to eat the Brahmana may break his sleep and spoil the stealing. The demon objected and said that he would eat the Brahmana first because any noise from stealing the cows may wake the Brahmana and spoil his mission. They started quarreling in stentorian voice which made Shivabhakta fully awake. Before the bewildered Brahmana could ask them anything, each of the quarreling thief and the demon disclosed to the Brahmana the intention of the other. Learning this Shivabhakta with Shiva Mantra made the demon flee and with a large stick chased the thief away.

Lessons: i) Dispute among the enemies is always advantageous for the protagonist.

35. The Serpent in the Belly of the Prince

Prakarkarna, a minister of the owls to his king Arimardana

The king Devashakti of certain kingdom had a son with some incurable disease. In fact the prolonged and debilitating illness of the prince was due to a serpent residing inside his belly. No doctor of the kingdom could diagnose the real cause of illness of the prince. So none could cure the prince and his condition went from bad to worse day by day. In deep despair and physical trouble the prince left home and in course of a long journey arrived at a new kingdom.

The king of that country had two daughters. Every morning the king used to meet his daughters. The elder daughter used to greet her father with praise and sweet words. The younger daughter, however, used to utter only one brief sentence, "You would get only the fruit of your labour." Soon this made the king very angry with the younger daughter. He ordered his men to take this girl out of the palace and give her to marriage with the first man they happen to come upon right outside the gate of the palace and make the couple leave his kingdom.at once. The moment the king's men with the daughter came out of the palace gate, they encountered the ailing prince who was then passing by the palace. So they got the princess married with the ailing and emaciated prince who in shabby garments, because of long travel, looked like a street beggar. The princess was given some money and a few maids and ordered the couple to leave the kingdom. The girl, however, considered this to be what she deserved in accordance with her deeds, and accepted her husband very gladly. She, with her husband and the maids moved on to a new kingdom. There she rented an abandoned house by the side of a river from a landlord and started living there with her maids and the ailing husband. One day when the maids had gone out for marketing and the prince was in deep slumber inside the house, the princess stepped out of the room and started strolling leisurely around the house. Soon she found through the window that a snake had come out of the nose of the prince. At the same time another snake came out from the mound in the courtyard and entered the room. The two snakes soon picked up quarrel. The snake from the mound blamed the other snake for causing illness to an innocent prince. The snake from prince's belly blamed the other snake for illegally occupying immense wealth inside the mound. In course of quarrel they disclosed the secrets of each other. From their quarrel the princess learnt that the snake in the prince's belly could be killed if he drinks decoction of black mustard seeds. Likewise the other snake could be killed by pouring hot water on the mound. After the maids had returned the princess ordered them to prepare decoction of black mustard. Thereafter she woke the prince and made him drink the decoction. The prince was fully cured in a few days. The maids also killed the other snake by pouring hot water on the mound. From the demolished mound the princess got a big box full of ornaments and jewels. This made them rich. Thereafter the prince and the princess lived happily.

Lessons: i) Those who cannot keep secrets are likely to perish.

36. The Chariot Maker Cuckolded by His Wife

Raktaksha, the owl minister to king Arimardana and other owl ministers

A chariot maker in a city had learnt from his neighbours about the infidelity of his wife. He wanted to find it out himself and catch her red handed. To this end he hatched out a plan. One morning he told his wife that he would have to go for some important business to a new town and he would return after one week. This information made the wife highly elated as she got the opportunity to have love game with her lover Devadatta for several days freely. As soon as her husband had left, the infidel wife went to the house of her lover Devadatta and informed him the matter and asked him to come to her bedroom at midnight through the main door which would be kept open.

The chariot maker spent the day moving randomly in a nearby town and returning in the evening sneaked into his bedroom through a side door and lay quietly under the sleeping bedstead. At midnight Devadatta entered the bedroom and got into the bed. This made the chariot maker extremely angry but he waited for the appropriate moment to catch the two lovers red handed. His wife got undressed and while going to ride the bed her toe touched the body of her husband. The intelligent lady could immediately anticipate the plan of her husband. But she was shrewd enough to fool her silly husband. As soon as her lover attempted to approach her in order to start love game, she moved away and said to Devadatta aloud, "Please think before you touch me. This morning while I offered worship to goddess Chandika as usual, I heard from the image of the goddess a warning that my husband would die in six months. I prayed to her to suggest some remedy against this impending misfortune. After my earnest prayer, the goddess suggested that if I can make love with another person only then the curse would pass on to that person and my husband would be blessed with a life of full hundred years. But before making love the person should be fully informed about the matter. This is why I have invited you here. Are you ready to make the sacrifice for the benefit of my husband at your own cost?" Devadatta understood everything and embraced the lady hard. The foolish chariot maker was elated to think that out of love for him and saving him from a curse his wife had been doing all these things. The pious lady had been taking so much trouble to save his life and to enable him to get the blessing of livelihood of full hundred years. So every movement of wild love game above gave him pleasure. After both the mad lovers had got exhausted in course of the orgy of wild love game they got dressed up and got down from the bedstead. The cuckolded chariot maker came out of his hiding smiling. He in ecstasy lifted his wife on one shoulder and the lover, who had sacrificed his own life for the benefit of the chariot maker, on another shoulder. It was already dawn and the fool went from door to door of the neighbours with the two lovers on his shoulders.

Lessons: i) Fools can always be deceived by deceitful maneuvres of cunning persons.

ii) Disaster befalls on the fool who showers honour on a person who ought to be punished.

37. The Mouse Maiden Who Weds a Mouse

Raktaksha, the owl minister to Sthirajivi the old crow

The great sage Yajnavalka, while returning from bath in the Ganges, happened to come upon a helpless female baby mouse escaped from the beak of a hawk. The mouse was still alive. The kind sage, by his yogic power, converted the mouse into a little girl and presented her to his childless wife. The wife of the sage was very happy to get this girl and brought her up with utmost care considering the girl to be her own daughter. As the girl reached the age of marriage the sage, at the request of his wife, endeavoured to find out an appropriate groom for the girl. He first thought of the mighty sun god. The god accepted the proposal of the great sage and agreed to marry the girl. But the girl declined the proposal claiming that the sun is too hot. As she expressed her desire for a better husband, the sage asked the sun god who could be better than him. The god suggested that the cloud god is better and more powerful than him as he is capable of overpowering the sun rays. The sage could get consent from the cloud god to marry the girl, but again the girl declined claiming that the cloud is too swarthy and ugly and she needed as husband someone better. At the query of the sage the cloud god said that wind is more powerful than him. But the girl claimed that the wind is of fickle nature moving randomly and she needed a better husband. The wind god said that mountain is more powerful than him as the mountain can resist wind. The girl said that the mountain is too hard and someone better is to be sought out for her marriage. The mountain said that the mouse is more powerful than him as it is capable of piercing through his body. As soon as the sage summoned a mouse boy the heart of the girl leapt in ecstasy. She requested the sage to reconvert her into a mouse maid and get her married to this mouse. The sage by his yogic power converted the girl to her earliest position, a female mouse. Thereafter the marriage ceremony was done pompously and the mouse couple went on living happily.

Lessons: i) Love for and attraction to one's own race remains intact under all circumstances.

38. The Golden-Turd Dropping Bird and the Three Fools
The owl minister Raktaksha to his loyal followers

A fowler happened to trap a bird which was unwary. Soon he found that the turd dropped by the bird turned into pure gold. This frightened him as he thought this bird could be some demon. Moreover, he would be arrested if the king learns that he possesses a gold producing bird. So the fowler went with the cage of the bird and presented it to the king detailing his experience with the bird. The king ordered his men to take proper care of the bird. At that moment the minister of the king said, "Your majesty, why do you believe this cock-and-bull-story of a superstitious fowler? It is not at all possible that a bird can drop golden turd. So please set this poor bird free." The discourse of the minister appeared convincing to the king. Without taking time to test the validity of what the fowler had said, the king ordered his men to set the bird free. After release from the cage the bird flew up to a high branch of a nearby tree, dropped a turd that soon turned into gold. Then the bird said, "At first I was a fool because of my lack of caution, then the fowler because of his superstition and later the minister and the king for lack of patience."

Lessons: i) Trouble resulting from foolishness of a person may at times be resolved by foolishness of others.

ii) A pack of fools are likely to invite trouble.

39. The Jackal and the Talking Cave

Raktaksha, the owl ministers to his kin and loyal followers

In a certain forest lived a lion named Tikhnanakh. One day he could not find any prey all through the day. In the evening he was very hungry. He still moved on in quest of some animal to be hunted to meet his hunger. Soon it was dark and the lion came upon a cave. He thought that the cave must belong to some animal. He entered the cave and lay inside quietly with the hope that the owner of the cave must enter his den at night. Then the lion would be able to kill him and meet his hunger with his flesh.

After some time a jackal, the owner of the cave, returned. He was very shrewd and cautious. So as usual, in order to check up if the cave was safe for him, he addressed the cave and said loudly, "Dear cave, I have returned and please greet me as you do every day." The jackal repeated the same request three times and as it was natural, there was no reply from the lifeless cave. Then the jackal expressed anger and said with grief in his voice, "Oh cave, you might be displeased with me and that's why you are not responding to my requests. This means you no longer like me. So I am now looking for another cave that greets me." At this very moment the lion roared loudly to greet the jackal. And the jackal in no time ran away as fast as he could.

Lessons: i) A cautious person can always avoid oncoming dangers through some tests appropriate for the specific situation he encounters. On the other hand, a person without caution dives headlong into trouble unawares.

40. The Cunning Serpent Who Carried Frogs on His Back

Sthirajivi, the old crow to Meghavarna, the crow king

In a certain place close to a pool lived a black serpent called Mandabish. There lived many frogs in the pool. But because of old age the snake did not have the power to chase and catch the frogs. To resolve the problem he devised a plan so that he could devour the frogs with very little effort on his part. So one day he lay like a very sick person close to the pool at a place clearly visible to the frogs. Soon this created attraction to a few frogs. They asked the reason for such weak and debilitated condition of the snake.

Mandabish replied that this was due to the curse of a pious Brahmana. One day while the son of the Brahmana was washing his feet in the pool the snake mistook his big toe to be a frog and bit it in order to eat the seeming frog. The boy died instantly. Soon the Brahmana appeared at the spot and cursed Mandabish for killing his innocent son for no reason. The angry Brahmana said to the snake, "Mischievous snake, you have killed my innocent son for no reason. I curse you that henceforth you would lose all power to catch your prey. You would have to carry the frogs on your back and live with whatever is mercifully offered by the frogs to you." Mandabish said that he was lying at that place in order to seek the permission of the king of the frogs to carry the frogs on his back. As the news was spread among the frogs they all got extremely elated to get the opportunity of humiliating their enemy by using him as vehicle of joy ride. The king of the frogs was also fooled like the other frogs and readily agreed to accept the proposal of the deceitful serpent. Thereafter a large number of frogs rode the back of the snake and those who could not find any space waited for their turn when some of the frogs would climb down to give them opportunity. The snake started moving very slowly. While the king of the frogs complained about his too slow motion, the snake said that for lack of food he was too weak to move fast. Then the king of the frogs permitted the snake to eat daily a few low grade frogs. The clever snake went on devouring frogs without any effort to his heart's content. The other frogs and their king could not realize this because the frogs were so numerous and all the frogs were obsessed with the pleasure of riding the snake-vehicle. One day another snake found Mandabish with the frogs on his back. When he said that what Mandabish was doing was inappropriate, Mandabish in a voice inaudible to the frogs on his back, told the other snake the story of the Brahmana Yajnadatta and His Infidel Wife. Then he left the place. In course of time the mischievous snake devoured all the frogs including their king.

Lessons: i) A cunning person may accept for the time being humiliating condition from his enemies in order to get them into his trust and destroy them in opportune moment.

40a. The Brahmana Yajnadatta and His Infidel Wife

Sub-story: The serpent Mandabish to the other Snake

In a city lived a Brahmana named Yajnadatta whose wife was of lose character and had many lovers. She used to prepare delicious sweetmeats for her lovers. Every day she used to go out to offer worship to the shrine of the great goddess close to the river Ganges. After offerings to the goddess she used to meet a lover at the appointed place.

She did all this after Yajnadatta had left home for service as a priest to a businessman. One day, he happened to return home early and had to wait for the return of his wife. To his queries about the reason for her absence from home, he infidel wife said that she had gone to give offerings to the shrine of the great goddess. The next day, in order to see what his wife actually did, Yajnadatta did not go to his work place and instead followed his wife secretly. Soon the wife reached the shrine of the goddess. She kept the major part of the sweetmeat at a hiding place and the rest near the shrine of the goddess. Then she went out and had a bath in the holy Ganges. In the meantime, Yajnadatta hid himself behind the image of the goddess. Returning from the bath the wife made offerings to the goddess and prayed, "Have mercy on me mother. Because of my husband, it is difficult for me to indulge in love with my lovers. So please suggest me how my husband could be made blind." Yajnadatta changed his tone and from behind the image said in a female voice, "I am satisfied with your prayer lovelorn girl. Offer your husband sweets made of butter and sugar every day at breakfast. He would soon become blind."

The wife happily went on doing so. After a few days Yajnadatta complained that he could not see anything at all. So he should soon have to get to another city to have treatment of his eyes. This made the wife ecstatic. She invited one of her lovers telling him about the blindness of her husband. The Brahmana pretended not to have seen the entrance of the lover to the bed room. Then while he was going to embrace his nude wife, the Brahmana entered the room with a cudgel in hand and started to beat the lover who ran away with a broken leg. Thereafter Yajnadatta chopped off the nose of his wife and forced her in that condition out of the house.

Lessons: i) Only an intelligent person can detect deceitful and improper activities.

Chapter-5: Tantra IV-Loss of Friendship

Primary Story: The Noble Monkey and the Henpecked Crocodile

By the shore of an ocean there was a bushy blackberry tree with perennial large, juicy and sweet fruits. There was only one resident of the tree, a monkey named Raktamukha. He spent his life happily being nourished by the juicy fruits. But at times he was afflicted with utter boredom and loneliness as he had nobody else to talk with. Fortunately, soon he got a friend. One day a crocodile named Karalmukha, who lived deep inside the ocean, happened to come to the shore of the ocean and lay under the blackberry tree with a view to taking rest. The monkey noticed the crocodile and addresses him "Hey crocodile, where have you come from and what are you doing here?" the crocodile replied, "My house is inside the ocean. I have come here to take some rest after long swimming in order to catch fish. My name is Karalmukha." The monkey told his name, offered the crocodile berries and soon they started dwelling on various subjects. They started liking each other. Since then the crocodile used to come under the tree every day and had talks with the monkey, satisfying his taste by the sweet fruits and taking some berries for his wife. The wife of the crocodile was very much fascinated with the sweet berries and all of a sudden an evil idea took possession of her thoughts. She thought that the monkey always takes this delicious fruit. So his heart would be extremely delicious and soon she felt an evil desire to gratify her taste by eating the heart of the monkey.

With this evil intention in mind she requested her husband to invite the monkey to lunch, bring the monkey inside the ocean on his back and thereafter kill the monkey so that she could savor the ambrosial heart of the monkey. At this the crocodile objected by saying that it would be a grave sin to kill such a good friend. Then his wife vociferously expressed her suspicion that her husband had declined because the monkey must be a female one and Karalmukha must have fallen in love with the female monkey becoming infidel to his own wife. Soon she threatened her husband that she would die by fasting unless her husband agreed to bring the monkey in mid ocean for killing him and extracting his heart. So at last the crocodile was compelled to agree to bring the monkey to mid ocean under the pretext of inviting him to lunch and fulfill the desire of his wife by killing the monkey and extracting his heart for the wife of Karalmukha.

That day the crocodile said to the monkey that his wife was very angry that he had not yet invited such a good friend like Raktamukha to their house for lunch. Moreover, she was also very eager to be acquainted with such a noble hearted person. He said with great modesty, "My noble friend, today your sister in law has arranged for your reception and a sumptuous lunch for you at our house. She has warned me that she won't let me enter home unless I bring you with me." The monkey said, "You are likely to live deep inside water. I don't know how to swim. So how can I go to your house?" At this the crocodile replied that they live on an island and he would be able to carry the monkey on his back. So unable to grasp the conspiracy behind this invitation the monkey got on the back of the crocodile. After coming to deep waters from where it was impossible for the monkey to escape, the foolish crocodile said with laughter, "My friend, make your last prayer to your deity as you are going to breathe your last soon." Then he disclosed to Raktamukha that he had brought the latter deep inside the ocean under the pretext of inviting him to lunch simply to kill him and extract his heart. This was a conspiracy to fulfill the desire of his wife who was keen on savoring the test of the delicious heart of the monkey. The monkey, although panicked under such an unexpected situation caused by the treachery of his trusted friend, did not lose his head. He laughed and said, "Oh my friend, you should have told me this earlier. Actually, I have two heats. This heart in my body is dry and tasteless. I have stored in a secret place on the tree the real juicy and delicious heart of mine. So let us return soon so that I may give you the real juicy heart. Also you need not have to do the sin of killing a friend in order to get the desire of your wife fulfilled." The crocodile, being fooled by the clever monkey, returned to the shore and the monkey did not waste a single moment to jump on to the tree. Then he said, "Nobody has two hearts. You foolish villain, now return home and never come to this place again. What a horrible person I had put my faith on!" The crocodile said smiling, "I was simply making a joke with you. Can I kill a friend like you? So, please come with me again and have lunch in our house." The monkey said that he could not be deceived twice. Only a fool after escaping from danger once again dives into the same danger. In this connection he told the crocodile the story of the Frog-King Gangadatta and the Snake Priyadarshan and that of the Lion, the Ass and the Jackal. Then he said that the crocodile had spoilt his conspiracy by disclosing his evil design to the monkey. In this connection he told Karalmukha the story of the Potter Mistaken as a Hero. The monkey said that the unlike the crocodile, nobody should trust a mischievous wife. He corroborated his view by the story of the Brahmana and His Mischievous Wife. Then to explain that a henpecked husband like Karalmukha is always subjected to ridicule, he told the henpecked crocodile the story of the Henpecked King and His Henpecked Minister.

While they were engaged in talks, an aquatic animal informed the crocodile that his wife had died of fasting. Only after sometime, while the crocodile was still lamenting for the loss of his wife, another animal informed that a large crocodile had captured his home. Then Karalmukha, in great trouble, sought the advice of the monkey. Raktamukha was at first reluctant to give the treacherous crocodile any advice. But at last his mind became soft and he advised the crocodile to regain his home by fighting heroically with the intruder. Karalmukha soon went back, fought hard with the intruder and regained his home by killing the trespasser.

Lessons: i) Friendship once broken can by no means be restored.

ii) It is a grave sin to deceive a trusted friend.

iii) Once it is revealed that a person is treacherous he should never be trusted again.

iv) A henpecked husband is a despicable creature.

v) Mischievous wives may bring about disaster in the life of the husband.

Secondary Stories

41. The Frog-King Gangadatta and the Snake Priyadarshan

The Ape Raktamukha to Karalmukha, the Crocodile

In a well there lived a frog king Gangadatta by name. A group of frogs revolted against him and started pestering Gangadatta and his relatives. In order to find some means to punish these unruly frogs Gangadatta came out of the well by means of the path made by the sides of the protecting ring of the well. He started roaming randomly and by accident saw a black serpent in a bill. The snake looked aged and incapable of moving fast to catch its prey. Gangadatta thought that he would get the wicket frogs punished by this snake. Gangadatta introduced himself to the snake and initiated conversation with him. He learnt that the name of the snake was Priyadarshan. Gangadatta disclosed to the snake his harassment by some unruly frogs and his intention to get them punished by Priyadarshan. While asked by the snake how the he could get entry into the well and where inside the well he could stay, Gangadatta assured Priyadarshan that he would show the latter the way leading to the inside of the well and a cozy place close to the water of the well for staying. Then the snake could easily catch frogs from the well. He requested the snake to catch only the frogs who were the enemies of him and not his relatives and followers. The clever snake agreed to the proposal. Soon Gangadatta took the snake down the path inside the well and showed him the place for his stay close to the water of the well. Thereafter he pointed out to the snake his enemies. Taking advantage of the folly of the frog king, the snake started eating frogs at his heart's content. Soon all the enemy frogs were exhausted and the snake started eating the followers and relatives of the frog king. He even ate the wife and children of Gangadatta. Under these conditions, in order to save his own life, Gangadatta said to the snake, "If you eat me now, there would be left nothing for you to eat. And it is very difficult for you to get out of the well on your own. So you would have to starve. I have already made a promise to you to arrange for your food. So please permit me to get out of this well and invite frogs from other wells under some pretext." The snake agreed to the proposal and Gangadatta escaped out of the well. When the frog did not return for many days, the hungry snake saw a lizard and asked it to find out Gangadatta and remind him of his promise. The lizard discovered Gangadatta in a pool and intimated him the message of the snake. Gangadatta smiled and said, "I have got the opportunity of escaping from a danger. I am not a fool to return to the well and face the danger again. So I would never again return to the well".

Lessons: i) A person who uses a deadly enemy to punish other enemies may himself be harmed by the enemy he utilized.

ii) An intelligent person, once freed from danger, never makes the mistake to invite the same danger.

42. The Lion, the Jackal and the Foolish Ass Lambakarna

The Ape Raktamukha to Karalmukha, the Crocodile

In a forest lived a lion named Karalakesara. He had a jackal attendant named Dhusaraka. Dhusaraka used to serve the lion by doing odd jobs for the latter. In exchange he got the leftover of the hunted animals after the lion had taken his part. Once the lion got involved in a fight with a bull elephant and was seriously injured, and hence was incapable of hunting. So both the lion and the jackal were at the point of starvation. Under such conditions, the lion asked the jackal to trick some animal to come within the reach of the lion who could then easily kill it. To carry out the order of his master, the jackal went out and after a long search he at last came upon the probable victim, an ass grazing on dry grass and looking very sad. The jackal asked the ass the reason for his sorrow. The ass named Lambakarna said that he had to work very hard for a washerman who did not provide him any nourishing food beside this yellowish tasteless grass. The jackal expressed sympathy for him and told him that he knows a place inside the forest with profuse green grass. Moreover there are a few beautiful young female asses who had requested the jackal to find a suitable husband for them. All these fooled the ass, especially the information about the female asses made him lustful. So he accompanied the clever jackal to the den of the lion who, out of haste, attempted to grab the ass before the latter was within the reach of the lion. The lion misses the ass who got panicked being attacked by a horrible animal and ran away as fast as he could. The Lion, missing his target, fell down on the ground. The jackal requested his master not to be so impatient and hasty. He promised to bring back the ass again and requested the lion to kill him at proper time.

The jackal again found the ass at the same spot. Lambakarna reprimanded the jackal for leading him to a ferocious animal. The clever jackal said, "Uncle, what a fool you are! It was not any ferocious animal but a female ass in marriage garments. She has got very angry with me as I had not given you prior information about her wedding robe of an ass bride. She has also vowed to fast to death unless I could bring you back for union with you. In fact she has fallen in love with you at first sight. So please accompany me again and get the desires of both you and the female ass fulfilled." The ass was once again fooled by the jackal and felt deep infatuation for the female ass. This time the lion did not fail to kill Lambakarna. And both the jackal and the lion had food for a few days.

Lessons: i) Obsession with females may put one into grave trouble. Any clever person can take advantage of this lust and infatuation.

ii) Only a loggerhead steps into the same trap for the second time after he had escaped once from it.

43. The Potter Mistaken as a Hero

The Ape Raktamukha to Karalmukha, the Crocodile

A potter named Yudhisthira once stumbled on the sharp edge of a broken pot and was seriously injured in his forehead. He recovered after some time but a deep long scar remained on his forehead. After a few years a great famine raged through the region. Many persons died of hunger. In order to save his life Yudhisthira left the place and after a long journey reached another kingdom which was free from famine. He soon got the job as a palace guard of the king. He was handsome and stout and therefore, he had no problem in getting the job. Moreover the scar on his forehead made the king believe that he must be a great warrior injured in some battle.

Now one day the king arranged for a ceremony to reward the veteran heroes on the basis of their valor. While the king asker the potter about his pedigree and the battle in which he had been injured Yudhisthira admitted that he was no warrior at all but a simple potter injured on forehead by a broken pot. The king then asked the potter to leave his kingdom immediately. The potter protested by saying that the king might taste his capabilities. At this the king smiled and said that a potter belongs to a different class than the princes and soldiers. So if the other soldiers could learn about his origin, they might kill him. In this connection the king told the potter the story of the Jackal Baby Reared by the Lioness.

Lessons: i) By revealing his real identity a person loses the gain offered to him on the basis of mistaken identity.

43a. The Jackal Baby Reared by the Lioness
Sub-story: The King to the Potter

In certain forest there lived a lion couple. One day while out for hunting in the forest the lion found an abandoned jackal cub. Out of kindness the lion picked up the cub by his teeth, brought it to his home and presented it to his wife. The lioness too felt compassion for the helpless jackal cub and started rearing him with her two cubs who were a bit younger than the jackal cub. The three cubs used to play together.

The lion cubs were yet to grow up enough to distinguish the jackal cub from them. One day while they were playing in the forest close to their home they found an elephant at some distance. The real lion cubs, out of their innate valiant nature, ran towards the elephant with attacking attitude. But the jackal cub, because of his hereditary nature, got panicked and fled back to home. After the elephant had moved in deep forest, the two lion cubs returned home and started ridiculing the jackal cub for his cowardice. This made the jackal angry and he was in a mood to fight with the lion cubs. The lioness immediately interfered and took the jackal aside. Then she disclosed that he was not a lion but a jackal and told him how they happened to get him and rear him out of compassion. Then she warned the jackal and told him to leave the place immediately because if her own sons are grown up enough to recognize the identity of the jackal, they would certainly kill him. Learning about his true identity the jackal got terrified and promptly left the place in order to find out his own race.

Lessons: i) One ought to live among his own race. Notwithstanding his qualities a person would never be welcome amongst persons of higher pedigree.

44. The Brahmana and His Mischievous Wife

The Ape Raktamukha to Karalmukha, the Crocodile

In a certain city an honest and noble Brahmana loved his wife deeply. But the wife was of mean nature and she always picked up quarrel with the other members of the family. She was also of lose morality and always eager for extramarital affairs. The noble Brahmana, however, could not assess the true nature of the lady because of blind love for her. Being fed up with the family quarrel the Brahmana left home and decided to get settled in some distant city. While the Brahmana and his wife were moving through a forest the wife was very much hungry and thirsty as she had not taken any food or drink for a long time. So the Brahmana requested his wife to take rest under a tree and he went out in quest of some village from where he could bring food and drink. Unfortunately he was a bit late to return and on return found his wife dead. He then started wailing for his wife. Suddenly from the tree, he heard a voice that said that the Brahmana could make his wife alive again if he offered her half of his own life. To do so he would have to announce thrice "I give half of my life to my wife". The Brahmana followed the direction and the wife was alive again. She took the food and drink brought by her husband and became well soon. Thereafter, they continued the journey. On their way they passed through many villages and small towns. But none appeared suitable for the Brahmana family for their habitat. One day they entered into a beautiful flower garden. The Brahmana asked his wife to wait there and he left for bringing food from the nearby village. When the Brahmana had gone away the wife found a cripple turning a water wheel and singing in a divine voice. The lady with lose moral character was charmed by his song and was obsessed with lust for the man. She promised the cripple that she would look after him if he made love with her. The cripple agreed and under a shade they made frantic love. After some time the Brahmana returned with food. The wife said that when the Brahmana goes away she gets none to talk with. She proposed that she would carry the cripple in a basket on her shoulder to get someone to talk with in the absence of her husband. The simple Brahmana accepted the proposal. One day when the Brahmana was asleep by the side of a well, the wife, with the help of the cripple, pushed him down into the well. Then she proceeded towards the city with the basket on her shoulder. The city guards checked the basket and discovering the cripple in it they took the lady and the cripple to the king. The lady complained the king with tears in her eyes that the cripple was her husband whom his bad relatives had tortured and made cripple and forced them out of the family house. Out of compassion the king gave them shelter. In the meantime the Brahmana, who could by luck, get out of the well alive, reached the king's court. Seeing him his wife said it was the Brahmana, who was the bad relative who had tortured her husband. The king, being misled by the corrupt lady, ordered death sentence for the Brahmana. Then the Brahmana told the real story and asked her wife to return what she had taken from her husband. Being forced by the king the ungrateful lady was compelled to utter thrice, "I give back what I got from my husband". As soon as she uttered this thrice she fell dead.

Lessons: i) Blind love for ungrateful wife brings disaster to the life of the husband.

ii) A woman of lose morality is always dangerous for her husband.

45. The Henpecked King and His Henpecked Minister

The Ape Raktamukha to Karalmukha, the Crocodile

King Nanda of an ancient Indian kingdom was a great king and his Prime Minister Vararuchi was a maestro in statecraft. Notwithstanding many laudable attributes the character of each of them was besmirched by a ludicrous flaw, viz. each was a plaything at the hands of his wife. The henpecked character made both of them virtual slaves to their dominating wives.

One day, in course of a quarrel, the wife of the minister expressed determination not to talk with her husband any more. Vararuchi fell to the feet of his wife and asked how he could allay her grievances. At this the wife said that she would withdraw her decision only if the minister shaves his head. The henpecked minister did so by calling on a barber to his house. Thereafter he started thinking how he could explain his ludicrous condition to the king and his court. But the problem was resolved soon. A spy of the minister informed him that the queen had humiliated the king by compelling him to play a horse and get the queen ride on his back. This information made the minister realise that he and his king were sailing in the same boat. So he shook off all feeling of shame and proceeded boldly for the royal court.

Lessons: i) Henpecked husbands, notwithstanding their attributes, are ridiculous to everybody. They may also commit activities unsuitable to their statuses at the behest of their dominating wives.

46. The Foolish Ass in Tiger-Skin
The Ape Raktamukha to Karalmukha, the Crocodile

The poor washerman called Sudhapada possessed an ass to carry the garments to be washed. He was too poor to provide adequate fodder to the Ass which became feeble and sick. One day, by luck, Sudhapada came upon a tiger skin, left by some hunter, inside the forest. Sudhapada picked up the skin and tried it on the ass. The skin fitted the ass well. Then Sudhapada had an idea of providing adequate fodder to the ass. According to his plan he got the ass dressed in the skin of the tiger making him look like a tiger and led the ass into the fields of the cultivators. The ass fed on crops at hearts content. Considering him to be a tiger the cultivators dared not interfere. Moreover, they thought that a flesh eating animal like a tiger would never do any harm to their crops. Every dawn the washerman used to bring back the ass. With nutritious diet the ass soon became plump and healthy.

One day, however, an unfortunate incident ended up the happy venture of the ass and his master. At midnight, while the ass was busy eating crops, he heard the braying of a female ass from some distance. The elated ass started braying in response to the braying of the female ass. The farmers then realized that they had been fooled by an ass in tiger skin. They soon came out with cudgels in hand and bit the ass to death.

Lessons: i) Foolishness may disclose the true identity of an imposter and put him into grave trouble.

47. The Infidel Wife and the Clever Thief
The Crocodile to the Ape

In a town there lived a rich old farmer. He had a middle aged voluptuous wife. The old man could not fully make his lustful wife satisfied. So the wife always went out to find some lover with a view to making love with him. One day while she went out to the market place in order to coax some young chap, her eyes got transfixed on a very handsome young man. In fact this person was a thief, waiting for an opportunity to steal something from a shop. The lustful glances of the middle-aged voluptuous woman made the clever thief realise the intentions of the lady. He soon got closer to the lady and said, "Oh lady, how beautiful you are! My wife had died recently and I have been looking for a suitable woman to marry. You are now my chosen person. I have fallen in love with you at first sight. Are you ready to marry me?" In fact the thief knew that the woman was the wife of a rich person and he was only after her wealth. But the foolish lusty woman could not realize the intentions of the thief. She agreed to elope with the thief early next morning when her husband would remain asleep. Accordingly she packed up in a bag all jewellery, money, and gems of her family as soon as her husband fell asleep that night, and in the next dawn left with the thief.

The thief chose a path that led to a river close to a forest. He had already learnt from the woman that she could not swim. Coming to a desolate place by the bank of the river the thief said that they would have to cross the river. He was unable to carry both the bag and the lady at the same time. So he would at first carry the bag and after his return carry the woman. He also made the woman agree to give all her clothes to the thief and stand nude by the desolate side of the river. The clever thief swam across the river with the bag containing wealth and did not return. Soon the woman realized that she had been cheated by the young man taking advantage of her obsession with lust. In the meantime, a vixen carrying a piece of meat saw a fish at the corner of the river. She left the piece of meat and ran towards the river in order to catch the fish. But she failed as the fish moved fast into deep waters. In the meantime, a kite swooped down and snapped the piece of meat left over by the vixen. The vixen then saw the nude woman, learnt her story and said to her that they had the same fate because of their folly of running after the shadow leaving the substance.

Lessons: i) One, who leaves the substance in order to chase the shadow, has always to repent.

ii) A person obsessed with lust can always be deceived by a clever guy.

48. The Silly Sparrow and the Ape

The Ape to the Crocodile

In a tree in certain forest there lived a sparrow couple. The hen sparrow had the bad habit of poking nose into affairs of other persons and pouring out unsolicited advice to persons even unknown to her. One winter day it was extremely cold and there was an untimely hailstorm. A monkey, in order to protect himself from the onslaught of the storm, took shelter under the tree on which the sparrow family had their nest. He was shivering in biting cold. The hen sparrow noticed this and true to her character, addressed the monkey, "Sir, you have hands like a human being. So like them you may build a house to protect yourself from this bitter cold. You appear to be a fool as you have not taken seriously the proper advice I have given you." The ape got very angry at this unsolicited advice, especially for the proud bird calling him a fool. Still keeping his cool he said, "Madam, I have not asked for your advice. So please mind your own business." The hen sparrow, however, did not pay heed to what the ape had said and went on pouring out her unsolicited advice. Now the ape expressed anger and warned the sparrow that if she goes on expressing her pride and audacity, he would not hesitate to break her nest. The proud sparrow still went on advising the ape. The ape then lost patience and climbing on the tree destroyed the nest of the sparrow couple.

Lessons: i) Unsolicited advice may not be welcome by the person advised.

ii) One who is in the habit of poking nose into the affairs of other persons may occasionally be in grave trouble.

49. The Cunning Jackal and the Dead Elephant

The Ape to the Crocodile

A jackal, looking for some food inside the forest, came upon a dead elephant. He felt ecstatic to find such a huge amount of food at a single spot. But unfortunately, he was unable to tear with his teeth the thick skin of the elephant. But he was very smart and thought that he would have to find some animal with stronger teeth to get the initial task of tearing the skin of the dead elephant accomplished. With this hope, he went on waiting at that place. Suddenly he found a lion approaching the spot. He bowed down at the feet of the lion and said, "Oh king, I have discovered this dead elephant and guarding it so that you may relish your hunger with this elephant." He did this just to please the lion so that the latter did not chase him away. He knew well that lions do not eat dead animals. The lion was pleased for the modesty and obedience of the jackal. He thanked the jackal and left the place. After some time, a tiger approached the spot. The jackal knew that if the tiger starts eating the elephant nothing would be left for him. So he said, "Tiger sir, this elephant has been killed by our king, the great lion. He has gone to take a bath in the river appointing me as the guard of the hunted elephant. He has also cautioned me that a tiger is likely to come to the spot in order to eat the elephant and in such a case, I should inform him by some signal so that he may return fast to kill the tiger and protect his food. So please leave this place at once in order to save your life." The tiger at once left the place as fast as he could. Sometime after the tiger had fled, the jackal found a leopard and beckoned him. When the leopard came close to the spot he clever jackal said, "Oh leopard uncle, you look hungry. So please pacify your hunger by taking one or two bites of flesh from this dead elephant. It has been killed by a lion who is now bathing. I have been entrusted with protecting this animal. But I think if you take only a few bites the hungry lion would not be able to detect it."

The leopard thought this to be a good proposal. But as soon as he tore the skin of the elephant the jackal shrieked, "The lion is coming. Please run away in order to save your life." The leopard fled promptly.

Then the smart jackal started eating the dead elephant through the wound created by the leopard on the body of the elephant. He once again got elated that this elephant would provide him food for a long time.

Lessons: i) An intelligent person can always resolve his problems and make an unfavourable situation turn favourable.

50. The Dog Chitranga's Bitter Experience
The Ape to the Crocodile

A dog called Chitranga lived in a city where there were very few dog lovers and the householders were very alert about the intruding dogs. So the dogs had to collect food with much difficulty. Under such conditions, Chitranga decided to leave the place and get to some city where food is easily available. With this decision, Chitranga left the place and after a long journey, he moved into a new city. There he found the house of a rich man whose wife was lazy and did not guard the kitchen properly. At noon, the lady used to sleep leaving the door of the kitchen open. Chitranga sneaked into the house through a crevice of the outside wall and remained hidden in a bush. At noon, when everybody in the house was asleep, he entered the kitchen and ate varieties of cooked food to his heart's content. The lazy and absent-minded housewife failed to detect the theft. So the dog passed two days happily stealing food from the kitchen of the house. In the third night, while he was roaming on the streets, relishing the sweet breeze after a sumptuous dinner, the local dogs, who could not tolerate any stranger, found Chitranga and attacked him. He was injured but could save his life by hiding himself inside a dilapidated house. After the attackers had left, Chitranga came out of the hiding and returned to his native city. The local dogs asked him about the new town and the reason for his wounds. At this Chitranga gave them the detail of his experience in the new city and insisted that food may be in plenty in foreign lands, but the local dogs there are inimical to a stranger.

Lessons: i) *Foreign land may provide amenities to a person not available in his native land. But the foreigners are not likely to welcome a stranger.*

ii) *Motherland is always superior to a foreign land even with better amenities.*

Chapter-6: Tantra V-Thoughtless Actions

Primary Story: The Stupid Barber and the Jain Monks

In the Indian city of Pataliputra lived Manibhadra, a merchant prince. In spite of his pious and honest living, by the cruel game of fate, his business was crashed and he became penniless losing all his wealth. At night he thought that this life of poverty had made him a worthless fellow because all power and honour depends on wealth alone. So he thought of sacrificing life by fasting. With these pessimistic thoughts, he fell asleep and soon got transported to the dreamland. In his dream, Kubera, the god of wealth, appeared before him and said that committing suicide is a grave sin. Manibhadra explained to the god the reason for his pessimism that led him to the decision to commit suicide. The god listened attentively to him and promised that the prince would soon be in possession of immense wealth by the blessings of the god. Lord Kubera said that next morning the god would endow Manibhadra with vast wealth in the form of a Nanga (naked) Jain monk. The god suggested that, as soon as the monk steps on the door of the house of the prince, he should hit with something hard the head of the monk. In an instant the monk would turn into a heap of gold coins that would enable him to be wealthy again.

The prince thought this to be a pure dream and illusion. But he was convinced that it was true while he found a naked tall Jain monk, as described by Lord Kubera in his dream, approaching his house. In the meantime a barber entered his house as requested by his wife for manicure of her nails. When the monk stepped into the house, the prince hit his head with a cudgel and the monk immediately got turned into a heap of gold coins. The barber was astonished to find the miracle. The prince took the barber aside, gave him some gold coins and requested him not to divulge the matter to anybody else.

On returning home, the barber started thinking that all Nanga monks are basically stores of gold. So he decided to be rich by killing the Nanga monks of the nearby Jain monastery. With this evil intention in mind, he went to the monastery, praised the monks with utmost modesty and invited them to his house. At first the monks had declined by saying that it was against the protocol of the monastery. But with the lure of much financial rewards and ancestrally obtained valuable ancient Jain texts written by Mahavira, the founder of Jainism, the mischievous barber could ultimately make the monks accept his invitation. The barber kept ready strong wooden sticks in order to hit and kill the monks. Next morning, as soon as all the monks had entered his house, the barber attacked them with the sticks. Many monks died instantly and the injured ones started crying desperately for help. The soldiers on guard of the city heard the shrieks of the monks and entering the house of the barber they readily saved the injured monks and arrested the barber.

In the court of the king the judges asked the barber the reason for his heinous activity. The barber gave detail of what he had seen in the house of Manibhadra who was soon summoned by the judges. Manibhadra disclosed to the judges everything since his miraculous dream. The judges ordered death sentence for the murderous barber.

Lessons: i) One should never undertake any action without having complete knowledge and information on the matter by means of thorough investigation and scrutiny.

ii) Even apparently greedless monks are not free from desires and they are therefore vulnerable to the offer of money and other worldly gains.

Secondary Stories

51. The Impatient Brahmani and the Faithful Mongoose

Judges of the King to the Merchant Prince Manibhadra

In a city, the wife of the Brahmana Deva Sharma gave birth to a male child. On the same day the Brahmana found a baby mongoose whose mother had died right after the birth of the cub. The Brahmana brought the cub home and the Brahmani started rearing the helpless mongoose along with her own child. The mongoose cub grew up fast as natural to a mongoose while the son of the Brahmana was still a baby. The mongoose was very faithful but still the Brahmani had apprehensions that it might harm her child as mongooses are predatory animals by nature.

One day the Brahmani was to go out to fetch water from the river at half a kilometer from their house. While going out she instructed her husband to remain at home until her return and see to it that the mongoose did not do any harm to the child on the cradle. The Brahmana, however, had no fear of the mongoose and he did not want to lose the earnings from his morning rounds of the houses of the disciples. So he left out leaving the child with the mongoose. As soon as he had gone out, the mongoose found a large snake approaching the cradle of the child. It soon attacked the snake and tore it into bits. His mouth was red with blood of the snake.

When the mongoose found the Brahmani returning home, he, with the hope of being praised for his heroic action, ran to the feet of the Brahmani who, seeing the blood on the mouth of the mongoose, thought that it had killed her child. In anger she hit the mongoose on his head by the water pot and killed him. Promptly returning home she found that the child was sleeping peacefully on the cradle and the bits of the dead body of a snake were scattered around. She understood her grave mistake and started lamenting for killing the faithful animal that was but a child to her. Soon Devasharma returned home with his alms bowl full of rice. He got shocked by learning about the unexpected incident. Then the Brahmani laid the responsibility for the misfortune on Devasharma. The sad incident could have been avoided if Devasharma could restrain his greed and stayed at home as requested by his wife. In this connection she told him the story of the Greedy Treasure Seeker and His Punishment.

Lessons: i) A person, who undertakes rash deeds on the spur of the moment without examining the details of the objective conditions, is compelled to repent.

ii) Excess greed at times may lead to unwanted incidents.

51a. The Greedy Treasure Seeker and His Punishment

Sub-story: To the Brahmana Deva Sharma by his wife

In certain city there lived four young Brahmanas who were close friends. The common problem of them was abject poverty as the father of each was very poor and they too could not find any means to earn much in the locality. However, each of them had a deep desire to become rich as they thought that everything could be obtained by wealth. And poverty deprives one of worldly comforts, social honour and everything notwithstanding his talents, education and inherent qualities. So the four friends started discussing how they could earn wealth. They browsed through various ideas and at last agreed to try their luck in foreign lands. With this in mind, they left home with whatever money they had. After some time they reached the city of Avanti. Here they bathed in the river Shipra and prayed to Lord Shiva in the Mahakala Temple. They continued their journey and learnt from some forest dwellers of a great sage named Bhairavananda with magical powers. Following the directions given by the local people they soon reached the Ashrama of the sage, and pleased him with their devotion and service. In response to their request of endowing them with magical power to earn wealth, the sage gave each a quill. He said that if a quill drops at any place, there would be wealth beneath the earth at that place. He also cautioned the four friends that excessive greed may lead to disaster. So they should return as soon as they get adequate wealth and should eschew limitless greed for wealth.

Thereafter the four friends continued their journey. Suddenly the quill of a friend dropped. Digging the ground of the place they found pure copper. The friend, whose quill had dropped, said that pure copper would enable them to provide adequate wealth. So he had no greed for anything more. He requested the other friends to share the copper and return home. The three other friends, however, desired to get something more precious. Soon the quill of the second fried dropped at a place where they got pure silver under earth. Now the second friend got satisfied with silver. But the other two friends proceeded in expectation of getting something more precious. Soon the quill of the third friend dropped and there they found pure gold beneath the earth. The third friend asked the fourth friend to remain satisfied with gold which would be divided between the two. The fourth friend was still desirous of getting something more precious, e.g. diamonds, rubies and other jewels. The third friend reminded him of the warning of the sage. But excessive greed forced the fourth friend to move onwards alone. After some time, he came to a spot where he found a man with a wheel whirling around his head. Blood was dripping from his head and he was in great agony. The fourth Brahmana asked the suffering man the reason for this condition. He replied that it was due to excessive greed like the fourth Brahmana. In an instant the wheel left his head and got around the head of the fourth Brahmana. Then the man told that because of over greed he got into this position thousands of years ago at the time of Lord Rama. And now that another person, viz. the fourth Brahmana with similar greed, had asked him the reason for his suffering, he was free and his punishment had been transferred to the fourth Brahmana. The man suggested that the fourth Brahmana would be free only if another greedy person asks him similar question and gets the wheel moved around his head. By saying this, the man left the place.

Soon the Gold-finder friend came to the spot in quest of his friend and found him in such a miserable state. He then got the detail of the incidents that led to the misery of the fourth friend. He reminded the suffering friend of his warnings at the spot of gold and insisted that by ignoring his warning the fourth friend had got into this condition of perpetual misery. The Wheel-bearer Brahmana asked his friend to give him company in course of his suffering. They exchanged some moral stories and the Gold-finder disagreed to accept the request of the Wheel-bearer and fled fast from the spot of the horrible wheel.

Lessons: i) Excessive Greed leads to disaster.

51a-1. Scholars Without Commonsense

Chain-story: Gold-finder to Wheel-bearer

In a city there were four young Brahmana friends. Three of them were great scholars with the knowledge of many yogic powers. But all of them lacked common sense. The fourth lacked scholarship but possessed commonsense unlike his scholar friends. Once, the three scholar friends decided to go to foreign lands so that they may earn wealth and fame by means of their scholarly powers. Two of them were unwilling to take along the ignorant fourth friend but the third scholar opined in his favour as he was a friend after all. When they were passing through a deep forest they came upon the skeleton of a lion. The three scholars wanted to test the efficacy of their yogic powers on this skeleton. The first friend had the power to endow a skeleton with flesh and blood. After he had successfully done so, the second scholar restored skin to the lion's body by means of his power. When the third scholar was about to endow life to the dead lion, the fourth friend with common sense requested him not to do so because once the lion was alive, it would attack and kill them. But the three scholars ridiculed the ignorant friend and the third scholar went on with the application of his magical power. The fourth friend, in order to save his life, promptly climbed up a high branch of the nearby tree.

Then as soon as the lion became alive, it killed the three scholars lacking commonsense. The fourth friend, saved by means of his commonsense, returned home after the lion had left the place.

Lessons: i) At times, common sense is more effective than scholarship.

ii) Scholarship without commonsense is likely to be useless and at times fatal.

51a-2. Thousandwit, Hundredwit, and Singlewit

Chain-story: Wheel-bearer to Gold-finder

In a lake lived two large fishes named respectively Shatabuddhi (Hundredwit) and Shahasrabuddhi (Thousandwit). They were so named because the former knew hundred tricks and the latter thousand tricks to come out of any trouble. They had a frog friend called Ekabuddhi (Singlewit) because he knew only one trick. They used to assemble together in the evening and get engaged in friendly gossips and discussions on various serious topics.

One evening, while they were engaged in conversation, they heard some fishermen who were standing close to the lake, discussing that the next dawn they would set large nets to this lake and catch all the fishes of the lake.

The frog thought that if a large net is set he too would be caught in the net. So he decided to leave the lake and take shelter in another lake through a connecting channel. For the situation he had this single wit only. He expressed his opinion to the big fishes and advised them that for safety they too should escape to the larger lake through the connecting channel. The fishes replied that it was an uncertainty that the fishermen would invade the lake next morning. On the basis of a mere possibility they were not ready to leave their ancestral home. Even if the fishermen set nets they, with the application of hundred and thousand tricks respectively, could easily escape. The frog, however, knew only one trick, i.e. to escape to the larger lake. So at night he with all his family members, escaped to the other lake.

The next morning, true to their discussion, the fishermen set in the entire lake large nets that enabled them to capture every living animal of the lake. The two large fishes were certainly among them. They applied all the tricks they knew but none could be of any use. The fishermen soon killed them with cudgels and sent them to the fish market. The frog with only one trick remained safe with all his family members.

Lessons: i) An appropriate trick is likely to be more useful than thousands of inappropriate tricks.

51a-3. The Jackal and the Singing Donkey
Chain-story: Gold-finder to Wheel-bearer

A washerman had a donkey named Uddhata. At daytime he had to carry clothes for the washerman. But at night he was set free to graze wherever he liked. One night while wandering in quest of food he came upon a clever jackal. Soon they became friends. The jackal suggested that they could, at night, break through the weak fencing of the cucumber fields of the peasants and eat cucumber at their hearts' content. Since then they used to spend their time happily eating cucumber at night. Once it was a full moon night. The moon light made the donkey ecstatic and he felt an urge for singing. Hearing about his intentions the clever jackal forbade him to do so. He warned the donkey that his song would wake the cultivators and this would lead to serious problems for both of them. At this the stupid ass got angry and said that the jackal was ignorant of music. Then he gave a long discourse on the science of music to the jackal and expressed his determination to sing some ragas appropriate for the full moon night. The clever jackal immediately fled to save his life. The foolish ass started singing inside the cucumber field. Raucous songs of the donkey made the cultivators awake and they soon captured the donkey. He was bitten heavily and then the peasants forced him to wear a heavy millstone around his neck. The donkey, with heavy weight around his neck and severe pain all over his body, could escape through the crevice of the fence and the jackal standing at safe distance started laughing by watching the reward the foolish donkey got for his singing.

Lessons: i) Activities at inappropriate time and place may lead one to jeopardy. But nobody can prevent a stupid from doing so.

51a-4. The Stupid Weaver and the Tree-spirit
Chain-story: Wheel-bearer to Gold-finder

In a certain village there lived a weaver named Sthulabuddhi (dull wit). He depended too much on the advice of his wife and did not undertake any activity without consulting her. Once his loom was broken and he was in need of timber for repairing it. So, with an axe in hand he set out and entered the forest in quest of an appropriate tree that could be felled for obtaining necessary timber. After some time he came to a beautiful place adorned with flowers and soothed by a gentle cool breeze. There was a beautiful tree surrounded by bushes. The weaver considered this tree to be appropriate for the necessary timber. But the moment he raised the axe to hit the tree, a voice from within the tree said, "Hey weaver, please don't demolish me. I am a tree spirit residing in this tree and enjoying the enchanting beauty and cool breeze of the place. In exchange for my life you may ask for any boon from me." The weaver replied, "Thank you tree-spirit for offering to bless me with a boon. But I am incapable of taking any decision on my own in this regard. So let me go to my village and consult someone about the boon that I may beg from you."

"O.K., consult whomever you like and let me know."

The weaver proceeded for his village and met a friend after entering the village. He detailed everything to the friend and sought his advice about the boon. The friend said, "Ask the tree spirit to give you a kingdom where you would be the king and I your minister. With this boon we would be able to enjoy power, wealth and all other conceivable worldly happiness."

The weaver said, "No doubt yours is a good suggestion. But I should also consult my wife in this regard before taking any final decision." At this the friend said, "N ever make that mistake my friend. A wise person never seeks advice from his wife." But the weaver, being too much dependent on the opinion of his wife, disregarded the warning of his friend and after going home related everything to his wife. The wife said, "Don't ask for a boon to be a king. A king is always overburdened with responsibilities and is beset with limitless enemies. Better ask for two extra hands and an extra head. Weaving by your first pair of hands on the front side would provide us income for facilitating provision of basic amenities. On the other hand, with the hands on the backside you would be able to earn enough to provide for luxuries."

The foolish weaver liked the advice of his wife and approaching the tree asked the spirit the boon of two more hands and one more head to his back side. The tree-spirit granted the boon. Thereafter the weaver with a happy heart proceeded towards his house. As soon as he reached the village people considered him to be a demon with two heads and four hands. Many fled away in fear and the brave ones started pelting stones at him. This ultimately killed the weaver.

Lessons: i) A wise man ought not to be guided by the advice of his wife.

51a-5. The Reverie of the Brahmana

Chain-story: Wheel-bearer to Gold-finder

A Brahmana named Swabhava Kripana (miser by nature) used to receive barley meals through begging. Every day he consumed a part of the alms received and stored the rest in a large earthen pot attached with a peg to the wall of his cottage. At night he used to lie under the pot and get obsessed in reverie. He used to think in semi wakeful condition that once this pot would be full with barley meals. Then a severe famine would hit the country. This condition would enable him to sell his barley meals at high prices. With the money obtained by selling the barley meals, he would buy a couple of goats. When the number of goats would increase through breeding he would sell them and by cows with the proceeds. He would soon have many cows and by selling them he would go into horse trading. His stable would be enriched with high pedigree horses and he would amass immense wealth. Soon a rich merchant would offer his beautiful and most accomplished daughter in marriage to Swabhava Kripana. Thereafter they would have a baby son.

One day when he would remain busy with the horses and his wife cooking in the kitchen, the child would crawl out of the house. Watching this, the Brahmana would shriek at high pitch to his wife to pick up the son. But the wife could not hear this because of the noise of cooking. So the angry Brahmana would pick up the son and going to the kitchen give a kick on the buttock of his wife for negligence and disobedience. One day while in reverie, his kick targeted at his wife's buttock hit the earthen pot. The pot was broken and all barley meals saved got spread on the floor and spoilt. In this way the reverie of the Brahmana ended up in frustration.

Lessons: i) Too much obsession with day dreaming ends up in frustration and pessimism.

51a-6. The Ogre's Necklace and the Ape's Revenge
Chain-story: Wheel-bearer to Gold-finder

The king Chandra of an ancient Indian kingdom was a lover of animals. To fulfill his hobby the king reared a troop of monkeys, a herd of rams and pedigree horses in his stable. One of the rams was a gourmand and used to enter royal kitchen to steal food items. The servants in the kitchen used to chase the ram away with a stick. One day, because of continued attempt by the ram to steal, one of the servants got fed up with it and out of utmost anger threw a burning log at the ram. Immediately the wooly body of the ram caught fire. The ram in panic entered the adjacent stable of the horses and started rolling on the hay in an effort to extinguish the fire in its body. Soon the entire hay stacked in the stable caught fire which killed some of the tethered horses and some others could escape with severe burns on their bodies. Soon the burns turned into painful sores. The king summoned the animal doctor who suggested that the only medicine to cure the horses is to administer monkey-fat in the wounds. To save the costly horses, the king ordered the soldiers to catch all the monkeys and kill them. The soldiers obeyed the order and killing all the monkeys extracted fat from their bodies. One old monkey, who had already escaped to a safe place on a tall tree near the royal palace, was saved. He had anticipated earlier the incident and had warned the other monkeys suggesting them to leave the palace and take shelter at a safe place. But they had simply ridiculed him. The loss of all his companions made the old monkey morose and also revengeful against the king who had killed all his monkey retinues and relatives. He started looking for some means to take revenge against the king. By good luck soon he got an opportunity to get his desire fulfilled.

One day while he was about to drink water from a lake he stopped short being cautioned by some ominous sign. He found human foot prints towards the lake but none out of the lake. This made him guess that there must be something wrong with the lake. So he collected a long hollow lotus stem and started drinking with it from some distance from the lake. Soon an ogre appeared on the surface of the water and the monkey was enthralled to find a beautiful ruby necklace adorning the neck of the ogre. The ogre said that he was pleased to the monkey for his presence of mind. In fact he cannot come out of water but eats all persons who enter into water. The monkey told his sad story to the ogre and also about his burning desire to take revenge against the mischievous king. To this end he asked the ogre to give him the necklace for some time so that he could entice the king and his mane into the lake. The ogre readily gave the necklace to be worn by the monkey. The old monkey started roaming in the palace of the king making the necklace visible to everybody. While the king enquired how the ape could procure it, the latter said that he got it by diving in the water of a lake. Anyone diving in that lake is entitled to be presented with such a ruby necklace. Next morning the greedy king, desirous of procuring a large number of such necklaces, followed the monkey with all his men to the lake. The monkey asked the king to wait on the bank with him and let only the men of the latter get down into the water of the lake first to procure necklaces. Later on they would dive into the lake. Accordingly all the relatives and retinues of the king dived into the water of the lake and were all devoured by the ogre. Finding their delay in returning the king asked the monkey the reason. The monkey said that they had been devoured by the ogre of the lake. He jumped on a tree branch and said that this was his revenge against the king who had killed all his men. So now let the king feel the pain of losing all his retinues and relatives.

Lessons: i) Advice of experienced senior persons should never be ignored or ridiculed.

ii) If a person is determined to take revenge, he would certainly get such opportunity at least once.

51a-7. The Princess and the Ogre

Chain-story: Gold-finder to Wheel-bearer

King Bhadrasen of an ancient Indian city had a beautiful daughter called Ratnavati. She was a paragon of beauty. A lusty ogre got infatuated in her and felt a strong desire to take her away. The ogre used to enter the room of the princess every evening and tried his best to carry her away. But he failed because of a divine protection ring around the princess. Failing to take her away, the ogre used to enter her body and made love with her, remaining invisible. This possession by the ogre made the princess feverish and she revealed other painful symptoms of possession by an evil spirit.

One afternoon while the ogre had just entered her room and was ready to take possession of her body, the tormented princess said to her maid, "Now it is Bikal (afternoon). Soon the mischievous ogre would enter my body and torment me. Can you please give me any suggestion how to get rid of this demon?" The ogre, who could not hear the princess properly, interpreted her talks to the maid wrongly. He thought that another ogre called Bikal takes possession of the body of the princes and tries to take her away. The ogre wanted to get the detail of the other ogre – his time of entrance, his power etc. In order to do so, he converted himself into a beautiful horse and hid himself among the horses in the adjacent stable from where he could see everything in the room of the princes. At mid night by coincidence, a horse thief entered into the stable by breaking through the door and after examining all the horses, decided to steal the most beautiful one, the ogre in the guise of horse. The thief then fit the mouth of the ogre-horse with bit, rode him and whipped his back hard in order to get away fast from the place. The ogre thought the thief to be the ogre Bikal and the hard lashing of the whip made him convinced that the latter was more powerful than him. So, with a view to saving life, he started galloping very fast. After coming to a safe distance from the palace, the thief tried to slow down the ogre-horse by drawing at the bit. But the panicked ogre accelerated his speed. The thief now thought that this could not be a horse but some demon instead. He, too, was panicked and wanted to be free from the back of the demon. Suddenly he found a tree branch within reach and jumped out of the back of the ogre-horse by catching hold of the branch. The ogre felt a relief being freed from the imaginary ogre Bikal. A monkey on the tree, a friend of the ogre, shrieked at high pitch, "Foolish ogre, why are you so frightened? This is but a human being. Return and kill him." At this the thief got angry with the monkey, held hard its hanging tail and started chewing it hard by entering the end of it into his mouth. The pain and unprecedented behaviour of a human being made the monkey bewildered. The expression of pain and fear in the face of the monkey made the ogre confirmed that Bikal was overwhelmingly more powerful than him and he fled at accelerated speed. In fear of the imaginary Bikal, the ogre never attempted to torment the princess again.

Lessons: i) Coincidence at times may play a crucial role in resolving a complicated problem.

51a-8. The Three-breasted Princess and the God of Fate

Chain-story: Wheel-bearer to Gold-finder

The queen of Madhusen, the king of Madhupur city, gave birth to a daughter with three breasts. The king consulted the chamberlain and other learned priests as regards what to do with this daughter with ominous signs. The council of the priests, after consulting the holy books, suggested that according to the provisions of the sastras (religious texts) the king should get this daughter reared in some secret place and once she achieves marriageable age, she should be given in marriage to anyone who wants to marry her for the reward of hundred thousand gold coins. Immediately after marriage the couple should be banished to some other kingdom.

As soon as the princess achieved the age of marriage, king's men announced with the beats of drums that if anybody agrees to marry the ominous daughter of the king, he would be rewarded with hundred thousand gold coins. But after marriage, he along with the princess would be banished from the kingdom of Madhupur. They announced that the willing person should beat the drum kept at a suitable place in the city.

In the city there lived a blind man with a hunchback to assist him. They used to live from hand to mouth by begging and were tormented by abject poverty. Hearing the announcement of the king's men, the blind man said, "If I agree to marry the ominous princess, it may lead to my death. Still, at least for the time being, we would be able to come out of this tormenting poverty and enjoy life with hundred thousand gold coins." The hunchback agreed with his friend. With this decision, the blind man sounded the drum. Soon king's men came with the princess and led the three at the bank of an inter-country river. There the princess got married with the blind man. The blind man was given hundred thousand pieces of gold as promised. Thereafter, the king's men made the three of them board a small fishing boat and ordered the boatman to drop them to some foreign country.

After sometime the blind, the hunchback and the princes were made to land in a foreign country. They soon walked to a small town and bought a good house for staying. Time went on and gradually the princess and the hunchback fell in love with each other and started making love secretly. After some time the two lovers wanted to get rid of the blind permanently so that they could marry and live a hassle free life. They conspired to this end and were in quest of some means to kill the blind man. One day the hunchback found a poisonous snake and killed it. He asked the princess to cut the snake into pieces, fry them and serve the blind man as fish fry. Eating the meat of the poisonous snake, the blind would die. The happy princess did exactly so and while the snake pieces were in the frying pan, she had to leave the kitchen for some time to attend some other family chores. She told her husband that she was frying fish for him in the pan and requested him to stir the fish pieces with a stick until she returns from attending other works. The blind man started stirring the snake pieces and the poisonous smoke, emitting from them, touched his eyes and his blindness was fully cured. Looking at the pieces in the frying pan he was astonished to find that they were not pieces of fish but that of a poisonous serpent. He was shocked to understand the evil intention of his wife and the hunchback. But he pretended to be still blind in order to detect the exact scheme of the two. Soon the wife along with the hunchback returned. She stored the fried snake flesh in a pot to be served to her blind husband at lunch. Thinking that they have almost achieved success, the two lovers, in ecstasy, started kissing each other as they could not know that the husband had already been cured of blindness. Soon they got into bed and started love making. The husband entered the bedroom and finding them in that game, he got vehemently angry. In a belligerent mood he caught one leg of the hunchback, lifted him high over his head and in anger started whirling him over his head. As he released the hunchback, his body forcefully hit the chest of the princess. At the heavy impact, the third breast of the princess was pushed in and the hump of the hunchback straightened out.

Lessons: i) The God of Fate is mysterious and nobody can anticipate His designs.

51b. The Brahmana and the Ogre

Second chain: To the King Madhusen by his Chamberlain

Once, a Brahmana was going to his disciple's house through a forest. All of a sudden an ogre jumped on to his shoulder and got settled there. The panicked and helpless Brahmana did his best to shake off the demon but the ogre was too strong to be got rid of. So the Brahmana went on walking with the demon on his shoulder. Now the intelligent Brahmana thought that physical force would be of no avail here. Better he would try to resolve the problem by means of intelligence. He started asking many questions to the ogre in course of gossiping. He thought that he could be able to learn the way out from the replies of the ogre. Through shrewd queries the Brahmana learnt that this person was a Yaksha. He had turned into an ogre because of the curse of a sage. He had also been cursed that he would die as soon as he steps on necked soil. So he could roam only on the grassy forest and now he had got the opportunity to come out of the forest riding on the shoulder of the Brahmana. After some time, they approached a lake. The ogre asked the Brahmana to drop him inside the lake so that he could bathe and offer prayers to his deities. Till the completion of his prayers the Brahmana should wait inside the lake.

As soon as the ogre started bathing, the Brahmana came out of the lake and ran away knowing fully well that the ogre would not be able come out of the lake as the banks of the lake were of naked soil.

Lessons: i) The way out of many problems could be found by asking and investigating.

Chapter-7: Lessons

Tantra I: Breaking off of Friendship

1. An ideal king should never be emotional and do anything in the spur of the moment.

2. An ideal king ought not to be gullible and should never be moved by the advice of a single person and he should discuss any report by someone with all his ministers and scrutinize himself calmly and applying political prudence. The king should always be cautious about vicious advice.

3. An ideal king should never budge from his royal duties and should never indulge in friendship, games, gambling or any such things that makes him negligent about his royal duties.

4. An ideal king should never behave like a coward and get panicked at anything strange or unusual as did Pingalaka by hearing the loud and strange bellowing of Sanjivaka.

5. Friendship between natural enemies, e.g. between a lion and a bull is not realistic and may not last long.

6. Unfair and conspiratorial means to achieve power ultimately leads to disaster for the conspirator as well as everyone else.

7. Seven evils that a monarch may be afflicted with: women, dice, hunting, drinking, abusive speech, rapine and imparting unreasonable severe punishment on any subject. These seven evils together are called addiction. The other fundamental evils that a king may be subjected to are: absence or lack of six requisites (ministers, land and subjects, fortresses, treasury, allies and punitive power).

8. One ought not to poke his nose into a matter which is none of his business.

9. One should not get terrified by sound alone, however strange and horrific it seems to be, before inspecting the exact cause and nature of the source of the sound.

10. Nobody should ignore the power of a person of lowly status if the latter has close access to a powerful person. Ignoring and humiliating such persons may bring about disaster.

11. One should never trust anyone, especially a newly acquainted person, while it involves matters related to treasures, property or wealth.

12. A go-between whether to take advantage of fight between two warring parties, or to assist any mischievous activity, or in other matter not related to his own business is likely to encounter doom.

13. A physically weaker person ought to resort to intelligence instead of physical strength to overpower a physically stronger enemy. Where physical vigor fails intelligence may provide a viable way out.

14. It is always helpful to seek advice from an intelligent friend.

15. Excessive Greed leads to doom.

16. Nobody should trust his natural enemy.

17. Intelligence is always more powerful than physical prowess and intelligence is likely to help to find a way out of any predicament.

18. Extraordinary strong will and determination may move even the gods of the heaven.

19. One should not ignore the good advice of benevolent friends.

20. One ought not to give shelter to a stranger about whose character one has no knowledge.

21. One, if happens to get into high position, ought not to neglect ordinary persons who had been close to him before he was raised to power.

22. Bad Company always invites trouble.

23. A powerful natural enemy with villainous counselors should never be trusted as a friend.

24. A person with mischievous associates should never be trusted.

25. One should not hurt and incur enmity of an apparently weak person without knowing his potential power.

26. Ignoring the advice of good friends may lead to disaster.

27. One ought not to ignore the good advices of the well-wishers.

28. Unity is strength. Weak persons, if united, can overpower a strong enemy.

29. Ancient people are likely to be wise and possessing experience. And so it is always beneficial to respect them and pay heed to their advices.

30. Weak persons ought not to disclose to the stronger natural enemies the activities that may identify their weaknesses and vulnerabilities. They should indulge in such activities in secret, out of the sight of the natural enemies.

31. A conscienceless cunning person is interesting in his own interest alone and in order to serve his vile purpose can always device means to deceive others.

32. A minister with wisdom of statecraft and diplomacy is one of the greatest assets of a king.

33. Word given should not be returned.

34. One ought to inquire thoroughly about the groom/bride before promising to offer his daughter/son to marriage.

35. None can reverse his destiny.

36. Nobody can teach a person who is determined not to learn.

37. Crime does not pay. A criminal son may incriminate even his parents.

38. No one should depend on the advice of a natural enemy as it may ultimately lead to his own disaster.

39. An unscrupulous person is accustomed to indulging in blatant lies in order to get his vile design fulfilled.

40. The character of a person depends a good deal on the cultural milieu in which he is brought up.

41. A noble foe is better than a foolish friend.

Tantra II: Pilgrimage for Friendship

1. True Friendship is more powerful than transitory material resources like wealth.

2. Friendship can be struck up among any persons irrespective of their class, creed, and category.

3. Persons with common interest should always cooperate with one another. Jealousy and rivalry in such a case may bring about disaster as in the case of the bharunda birds.

4. In the mundane world wealth is the source of power of a man. A man with wealth is respected in the society irrespective of his qualities.

5. People are attracted to a wealthy person and accept him as leader easily.

6. Once a person loses his wealth, he loses his power and his followers and dependants abandon him.

7. Unusual behaviour contrary to the nature of a person always has some hidden reason behind it. And therefore this type of behaviour of a person should always be suspected and dealt with caution.

8. Excessive greed leads to disaster.

9. What a man would get in life is pre-destined and nothing can change this. One in his life would get neither more nor less than what is fixed by destiny for him.

10. Fate is the final deciding factor as regards what a person would earn. If luck is against a person, he may not be able to earn much in spite of utmost efforts. Even if earned it would be lost. On the other hand, if fate is in favour, a person would be able to earn much with very little effort. In brief, achievement in life of a person ultimately depends on his destiny.

11. Wealth as such has attraction to most of the persons. Whether it is procurable or not people still hang around wealth.

12. Small and apparently insignificant persons could be of help to a powerful person under certain circumstances. So, one should not hesitate to strike up friendship with any person with a good heart but apparently less powerful or insignificant as compared to him.

13. Inadvertence may lead to trouble. Fate also may be responsible for predicaments. But with the help of intelligent friends and with appropriate planning, problems could be overcome.

Tantra III: War of Attrition between the Crows and the Owls

1. Diplomacy and intelligence are more powerful than physical strength.

2. One should never trust and give shelter to an agent of his natural enemy.

3. Inadvertent activity and silly deeds at the spur of the moment may lead to permanent harm like creating permanent natural enemies.

4. A shrewd person can easily fool an enemy much powerful than him.

5. Simply the mention of God makes many persons frightened and prevents them from undertaking mischievous activities.

6. A ferocious and deceitful animal or person like a cat should never be trusted.

7. A third party with criminal intentions can easily take advantage of dispute of two persons.

8. Repeated lies may make falsehood appear true. So a person could be deceived by repeated lies from different persons with prior conspiracy.

9. A strong person can be overpowered and destroyed by weak persons who are united and innumerable.

10. Love and Friendship once broken can by no means be restored.

11. Selfishness and jealousy are baser attributes of character and should always be avoided.

12. A noble soul possesses kindness and compassion even for his enemy.

13. Advantage obtained even from an unwanted person should always be welcome

14. Dispute among the enemies is always advantageous for the protagonist.

15. Those who cannot keep secrets are likely to perish.

16. Fools can always be deceived by deceitful maneuvres of cunning persons.

17. Disaster befalls on the fool who showers honour on a person who ought to be punished.

18. Love for and attraction to one's own race remains intact under all circumstances.

19. Trouble resulting from foolishness of a person may at times be automatically resolved by foolishness of others.

20. A pack of fools are likely to invite trouble.

21. A cautious person can always avoid oncoming dangers through some tests appropriate for the specific situation he encounters. On the other hand, a person without caution dives headlong into trouble.

22. A cunning person may accept for the time being humiliating condition from his enemies in order to get them into his trust and destroy them in opportune moment.

23. Only an intelligent person can detect deceitful and improper activities.

Tantra IV: Loss of Friendship

1. Friendship once broken can by no means be restored.

2. It is a grave sin to deceive a trusted friend.

3. Once it is revealed that a person is treacherous he should never be trusted again.

4. A henpecked husband is a despicable creature.

5. Mischievous wives may bring about disaster in the life of the husband.

6. A woman with lose moral character is occasionally ungrateful and dangerous for her husband.

7. A person who uses a deadly enemy to punish other enemies may himself be harmed by the enemy he utilized.

8. An intelligent person, once freed from danger, never makes the mistake to invite the same danger.

9. Obsession with females may put one into grave trouble. Any clever person can take advantage of this lust and infatuation.

10. Only a loggerhead steps into the same trap for the second time after he had escaped from it.

11. By revealing his real identity, a person loses the gain offered to him on the basis of mistaken identity.

12. One ought to live among his own race. Notwithstanding his qualities a person would never be welcome amongst persons of higher pedigree.

13. Blind love for ungrateful wife brings disaster to the life of the husband.

14. A woman of lose morality is always dangerous for her husband.

15. Henpecked husbands, notwithstanding their attributes, are ridiculous to everybody. They may also commit activities unsuitable to their statuses at the behest of their dominating wives.

16. Foolishness may disclose the true identity of an imposter and put him into grave trouble.

17. One, who leaves the substance in order to chase the shadow, has always to repent.

18. A person obsessed with lust can always be deceived by a clever guy.

19. Unsolicited advice may not be welcome by the person advised.

20. One who is in the habit of poking nose into the affairs of other persons may occasionally be in grave trouble.

21. An intelligent person can always resolve his problems and make an unfavourable situation turn favourable.

22. Foreign land may provide amenities to a person not available in his native land. But the foreigners are not likely to welcome a stranger.

23. Motherland is always superior to a foreign land even with better amenities.

Tantra V: Thoughtless Actions

1. One should never undertake any action without having complete knowledge and information on the matter by means of thorough investigation and scrutiny.

2. Even apparently greedless monks are not free from desires and they are therefore vulnerable to the offer of money and other worldly gains.

3. A person, who undertakes rash deeds on the spur of the moment without examining the details of the objective conditions, is compelled to repent.

4. Excess greed at times may lead to unwanted incidents and disaster.

5. At times, common sense is more effective than scholarship.

6. Scholarship without commonsense is likely to be useless and at times fatal.

7. An appropriate trick is likely to be more useful than thousands of inappropriate tricks.

8. Activities at inappropriate time and place may lead one to jeopardy. But nobody can prevent a stupid from doing so.

9. A wise man ought not to be guided by the advice of his wife.

10. Too much obsession with day dreaming ends up in frustration and pessimism.

11. Advice of experienced senior persons should never be ignored or ridiculed.

12. If a person is determined to take revenge, he would certainly get such opportunity at least once.

13. Coincidence at times may play a crucial role in resolving a complicated problem.

14. The God of Fate is mysterious and nobody can anticipate His designs.

15. The way out of many problems could be found by asking and investigating.

————————————XXXXXXX————————————